ALMOST FA

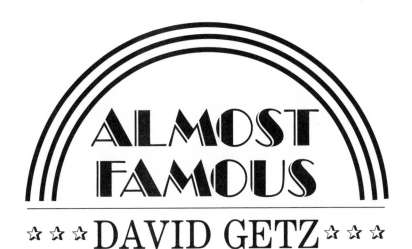

# ALMOST FAMOUS

★ ★ ★ DAVID GETZ ★ ★ ★

HENRY HOLT AND COMPANY • NEW YORK

First edition
Published by Henry Holt and Company, Inc.,
115 West 18th Street, New York, New York 10011.
Published simultaneously in Canada by Fitzhenry & Whiteside Ltd.,
91 Granton Drive, Richmond Hill, Ontario L4B 2N5.

Library of Congress Cataloging-in-Publication Data
Getz, David.
  Almost famous / David Getz.
  Summary: Ten-year-old Maxine is determined to become a famous inventor
so she can take care of her younger brother's heart condition, and she con-
vinces a troubled classmate to help her.
  ISBN 0-8050-1940-5 (alk. paper)
  [1. Brothers and sisters—Fiction. 2. Inventors—Fiction. 3. Schools—Fic-
tion.]  I. Title.
PZ7.G3299Al  1992    [Fic]—dc20      92-25755

Printed in the United States of America
on acid-free paper.∞

10  9  8  7  6  5  4  3  2  1

For my father,
who always gave me a choice:
story by book or story by mouth.

I would also like to thank
my ever lovely wife, Jacqui,
my mom and my sister,
and of course, Maxine Gillian,
who will always get a choice:
story by book or story by mouth.

☆ ☆ ☆

# Contents

# ALMOST FAMOUS

# ☆ 1 ☆

# The Room Was Dark

## *March 10*

The room was dark. Maxine watched the monitor start up and give off a blue glow. In a minute, it would show a picture of her brother's heart.

Their mother sat on a stool by her brother's head, her elbows on the examination table, her chin in her hands. Her black hair fell about her face. "So, what do you want to hear?" their mother whispered to Wat. "A story about a good knight or a bad knight?"

"Bad knight," Wat said, unexcited.

Doris, the technician, punched instructions into the echocardiograph's computer. She had thick fingers. She was tall, with wide shoulders and curly red hair. Standing over Wat, she looked like a fairy-tale giant.

"Once upon a time," their mother whispered, "there was a knight who was so bad, his armor was made out of tinfoil, and his horse had training wheels."

Wat lay quietly on the examination table. His brown

eyes, his tiny nose, his soft cheeks glowed in the light from the monitor. His chest and little belly, painted blue from that light, rose and fell with his nervous breaths. Maxine leaned against the table and squeezed her brother's hand. She didn't want to look at his eyes. They were wide open and fearful.

She glanced back over her shoulder at their father. He was standing in the light of the partially opened door, his jacket unzipped, his hands in his pockets. He mouthed the words, "Don't worry," and winked, and waved the worry away, as if it were a small fly pestering him.

"I don't like it here anymore," Wat said.

Their mother stroked Wat's hair. "Don't you want to hear about the bad knight? He was so scared of the dark, he slept with a *knight* light."

"It's not fun," he said.

"Just pretend," their mother whispered, "you're the brave knight."

"I want to go home," Wat said.

"Soon," she told Wat. "You love castles. Pretend this is just a dark castle."

"I'm scared," Wat explained.

"Just a few more minutes," their mother reassured him. "Be my brave knight, Wat. We're all here."

Maxine looked down at her hand, which had turned blue and strange, holding Wat's fingers. Thin white cables were fastened to Wat's chest and sides by sticky pads. Maxine traced the cables back to the machine's console. The monitor still displayed a blank, blue screen. Soon, it was going to show Wat's heart.

How did it work? She had read the pamphlet over and over. Something about sonar. A microphone was attached by a cable to the computer. It sent sound waves deep into Wat's chest, which bounced off his heart and back into the microphone. The computer somehow turned those sound waves into pictures. Maxine wondered what she had at home that could create sound waves.

Doris squeezed a gel onto the tip of the microphone and pressed a button. The microphone gave off a gentle hum. Maxine felt her heart begin to race.

Their father walked toward them. He leaned over their mother, and whispered something in her ear. He kissed her.

"Wat," their mother said, glancing up at the monitor, then back to Wat, "this knight was so bad, he used a butter knife for a sword. His dragons lived in pet shops."

"Maxine," Wat said, "I want to go home." He began to squirm.

"Now, Wat," Doris said, "you're going to have to lie still."

"Maxine," Wat whispered, "I don't want to do this anymore."

"But Wat," Maxine whispered back, trying to sound cheerful, "it's a great invention. It's not going to hurt a bit."

"I know," Wat said. "I know. I did it before, and before, and before."

"It uses sonar," Maxine said, "like they use on ships to see what's in the ocean beneath them."

"I don't care," Wat said.

"Yeah," Maxine joked, looking up at her parents, "well, what if they find a school of fish swimming around inside your ribs? Or buried treasure?"

"Now *that* would be something to worry about," their father said.

"I don't care," Wat insisted. He started to squirm again.

"Wat," Doris urged, "you have to lie still."

Doris slid the microphone wand under and across Wat's ribs. She stopped and pressed some buttons on the computer's keyboard. Red and blue flashes appeared on the monitor, shooting in and out of curved gray shadows.

"That's his heart?" Maxine asked Doris. It looked like pieces of a jigsaw-puzzle moon.

"Yup," Doris said.

Maxine studied the screen. The moon was pulsing, shooting out red and blue sparks. What was it showing? What was the picture telling her? Was his heart getting worse?

"What are you looking at, Maxine?" Wat asked.

"Wat," she said, peering at the screen dramatically, "remember those dinosaur erasers I brought you that you lost?"

"Yeah."

"Lie still, Wat," Doris urged.

"I can see . . ." Maxine leaned closer to the screen, "two of them in the picture. A stegosaurus and a . . . brontosaurus."

"No, you can't," Wat argued.

"It looks to me like you swallowed them whole," Maxine said.

"I did not."

"Shh, Wat, don't fidget," Doris repeated. "You're going to ruin the test."

"I want to go home," Wat said, beginning to cry.

Their mother patted his head. "Just another few minutes, Wat," she promised. "Do you want to hear more about the bad knight? He always had to get a note from his mother before he went on any adventures."

"I want to go home."

Doris turned to their parents. "If he doesn't stay still, we'll have to give him chloral hydrate and put him to sleep."

Their mother leaned over and kissed Wat's forehead. "Lie still, honey. Lie still."

Except for the hum of the machine and the sound of Doris clicking buttons, the room became quiet. Maxine watched Doris complete the examination. She stared at the curved, shadowy shapes shifting and changing. Doris pressed another button. As the red and blue flashes shot in and out of the shadows, the monitor produced the sounds of Wat's heart—its *woosh woosh,* and a strange whistling sound.

What does it all mean? Maxine wondered. What if something is worse with Wat's heart? Could they fix it?

"Done!" Doris sang out. "Good boy!" She began to peel off the sticky tabs from Wat's chest.

Wat sat up on the table. Their mother and father helped him on with his shirt. Maxine studied their mother's face. She was forcing a smile. Her eyes were red.

Maxine turned to Doris. "It's an amazing invention," she said.

"It is, isn't it?" Doris answered, punching some keys on the computer's keyboard. "It can see all sorts of things."

"Who invented it?" Maxine asked.

"Don't know," Doris said, shrugging. "But I wish it was me."

"Me too," Maxine agreed.

Doris smiled and punched two more keys. She removed a videocassette from the top of the machine.

"Mr. and Mrs. Candle, Dr. Stone will be with you in a few minutes. You can go back to the waiting room."

"I want to go home," Wat said as their mother buttoned his shirt.

Maxine looked up at the monitor. It was blank. Her brother's heart was gone.

Who had invented the echocardiograph? Who had

invented any of these amazing machines that helped Wat? They didn't even know Wat. How did they know what he needed? How did they know what to invent?

Suddenly Maxine became frightened. What if one day Wat needed her to invent something? What could she invent? A heart was a difficult thing to understand. But she knew her brother—she knew him better than any of those inventors. There had to be something she could do.

# ☆ 2 ☆

# Maxine Invents

## Later That Same Day

Back in Dr. Stone's waiting room, Maxine glanced over at the blocks corner, where Wat was fastening one colored cube to another. He wanted to be left alone. He was building a castle. Wat was always building castles. At bedtime, Wat asked their mother or father for stories about knights and dragons, and each day Wat built a new castle. Maxine returned her attention to the book on heart disease she had taken out of the library. She studied the description of the echocardiograph.

She never could have invented it herself. Not at home, at least. It had used a computer, a video monitor, and a microphone to make a movie of Wat's heart. She had been so excited to see it work. Why did inventions for Wat have to be so complicated? She leaned over to her father.

"Dad, explain sonar. I understand that the echocardiograph uses sonar. But how does sonar work?"

Maybe if she understood sonar, she could build something almost like an echocardiograph at home. "How?"

"Mr. and Mrs. Candle?" a woman called. "Dr. Stone will see you now."

She watched her parents follow the woman down a corridor. Maxine glanced back down at the picture of the echocardiograph. It was another invention for Wat.

She remembered them all. When her mother was pregnant with Wat, five years ago, Maxine had gone with her for one of her checkups. The invention used on that day was a sonograph. Holding her mother's hand, Maxine watched as a pretty, short-haired woman ran a wand over her mother's belly. Shadowy images appeared on a monitor.

"That's your brother, Maxie." Her mother laughed, pointing to the monitor.

"How?" was all she could ask. All she could see were fuzzy gray shapes. She was only five.

"This microphone," the technician explained, holding up the wand, "can see inside your mommy's belly." Standing on her tiptoes, Maxine pressed her eye to her mother's belly. She couldn't see anything.

The woman and her mother laughed. For the next few days, Maxine went around the house, looking for different objects to press against her mother's belly. She tried carrots, bananas, a paper-towel roll, and a telescope. She wanted to see her brother.

A month later, her mother was in the hospital. Her

father told Maxine not to worry. Everybody was going to be fine. A nurse placed a strap across her mother's belly. The strap was attached to a machine that drew squiggly lines on a roll of paper. The machine was called a fetal-heart monitor.

"We're watching your brother's heartbeat," her father told her, staring nervously at the squiggly lines.

"Why?"

"To make sure he stays healthy," her father explained.

That evening, when her mother was sleeping, the nurse was out, and her father was downstairs in the hospital's cafeteria, Maxine placed her belt over her mother's belly.

"Maxie, what are you doing?" her mother asked, sounding groggy.

"Shhh, I'm listening to the baby," she said. "I'm keeping him healthy."

The next day, Wat was born. He was skinny, wrinkled, pink, and wet, with a big head and bulging eyes. He wouldn't stop crying.

Looking through the window of the nursery, Maxine asked her mother to bend down. She had a secret.

"What is it, dear?" her mother asked.

"I don't think he's ready yet," Maxine whispered. "I think you should put him back in."

"Oh, I don't think your father would like that," her mother said, smiling.

"What is that for?" she asked, pointing to the clear plastic box that contained her brother.

"That's to keep him warm," her mother said.

"See!" Maxine pointed out. "I'm right. He's not ready yet. I think you should put him back in."

The next day in school, Maxine's kindergarten teacher asked her what she was building in the blocks corner.

"An oven," she told Mrs. Zweig.

"To bake bread?" Mrs. Zweig asked.

"No, to keep my baby brother warm," she answered.

A few weeks later, her parents took Wat for his first checkup with Dr. Klein, who was also Maxine's pediatrician. Using a stethoscope. Dr. Klein listened to Wat's chest and heard a funny sound. "A murmur," Maxine heard Dr. Klein tell her mother. "Nothing to get scared about." Dr. Klein suggested to her parents that they take Wat to Dr. Stone.

Maxine insisted on going with them. She was afraid they were going to give Wat back to the hospital.

"Maxie, he's here for good. Wat's going to grow up with you." Her mother smiled. "He's going to need you to teach him so many things. You're going to be his hero. He's going to be your little brother forever."

She remembered what he looked like when he was born. She remembered the sonograph and the fetal-heart monitor. "I want to go."

Her father suggested she stay with their neighbor. Maxine threw a tantrum. Her parents took her.

After Dr. Stone's examination, while her parents changed Wat's diaper, Maxine followed Dr. Stone into his office.

"What's a murmur?" she asked, surprising him. He turned around.

"It's a little sound," Dr. Stone said, patting Maxine's head. "It comes from a tiny hole in his heart. A teeny, tiny hole."

"We're not going to have to give him back to the hospital?"

"No."

"He's not going to die?" she asked.

"No, no, no," Dr. Stone insisted. "Here, listen," he said, taking the stethoscope off his shoulders and placing the two hearing plugs in Maxine's ears. "The stethoscope is a truly wonderful invention," Dr. Stone said, making the word *invention* sound magical, like a secret between them, like a birthday surprise. "It makes the sound of a person's heart much louder. Listening with a stethoscope is called ..." He paused and smiled. "Can I teach you a big word, Maxine?"

"Yes," she answered.

"Listening with a stethoscope is called auscultation. Here." He placed the silver disk of the stethoscope over his own chest.

*Lub-dub, lub-dub, lub-dub.*

"When I listen to Wat's heart," Dr. Stone explained, gently removing the stethoscope from Maxine's ears, "I hear what you just heard, along with a little whistling sound. That just means Wat has a small hole in his heart."

"He's not sick?" Maxine asked.

"Nope," Dr. Stone said confidently. "And all I need to do is listen to him from time to time."

"With your stethoscope?" Maxine asked.

"That's really all I need." Dr. Stone smiled. "There are other inventions I'll want to use, just to double-check. The stethoscope is still the best. I think it was invented just for Wat."

That afternoon, in their large apartment on Manhattan's Upper West Side, Maxine tried to make her own stethoscope. She used the tubing from her parents' aquarium.

"Maxine!" her mother shouted, pointing to the bubbling, muddy fish tank. "What did you do?"

"I made an invention for Wat," she said.

"You got water all over the floor."

"I just wanted to listen to his heart, Mommy."

"Oh, Maxine." Her mother sighed, peering into the tank. "I think two of the fish are going to need your help before Wat does. Honey, please stop worrying about your brother."

"But this is an invention," she explained.

"Why don't you just play with some of your toys? You have so many toys."

Maxine didn't give up. A year later, when Wat first showed an interest in walking, Maxine stuffed paper towels, clay, and wires into Wat's baby boots to keep his ankles stiff enough to allow him to stand.

"It's not really safe, Maxine," her mother said, holding Wat on her lap and carefully removing the wires from inside his boots. "You shouldn't play with wires."

"But it's a walking invention!" she explained.

"Maxine, you really don't need to worry. Wat will walk when he's ready," her mother explained. "Why don't you just play 'dress-up'? Isn't he fun just to dress up?"

When Wat started suffering from ear infections, Maxine stuck cotton balls inside of coffee filters inside of two Styrofoam cups.

"It's an ear protector invention!" she announced to her father.

"Maxine," her father said, delicately removing the cotton from Wat's ears, "it's not really a good idea to put things into a baby's ears."

"I didn't want him to get any more earaches."

"Maxine," her father said, "why don't you teach Wat to stop eating the refrigerator magnets?"

When Wat was three and her family had moved from their Manhattan apartment to a smaller one in Queens, she overheard her parents wondering why Wat wouldn't eat apples, or pears, or bananas. Maxine spent a few days mixing gum, licorice, jam, and candle wax into thin strips.

"It's a bandage for bruised fruit," she showed her parents.

"Maybe," her father said, as he peeled the waxy strips from a Red Delicious, "it's just a stage she's going through."

"Maxie, you really don't have to worry about Wat going hungry, or getting scurvy," her mother said. "He does drink juice."

"It was an invention," Maxine explained.

"Maybe," her father guessed, tasting the strip then spitting it out into a napkin, "you think she could be gifted? Maybe this is what gifted children do. Maybe we could try her on a musical instrument. Maxie, how would you like to learn how to play the flute?"

"The flute is already invented," she answered.

Only Dr. Stone treated her like an inventor. She had snuck in to see him twice since the day he had promised her they weren't going to return Wat to the hospital. Both times her parents were distracted, busy changing or feeding Wat. She showed him drawings of her ideas. He examined them closely, as if he were looking at a patient's X ray.

"It doesn't work," she said the last time, showing him her drawing for whistling sneakers. "I wanted to invent something that would make Wat's feet sing as he ran."

"Well, it looks as if it almost works," he said, studying her sketch.

"It's always almost," she complained.

"Maxine, Edison tested two thousand different filaments for his incandescent bulb before he discovered tungsten."

"What's tungsten?" she asked.

"Study your inventors, Maxine," he said. "And remember what Newton said when they asked him how he made his discoveries. 'By keeping the problem constantly before my mind.' Don't give up. One day you're going to invent something for Wat," he promised her, "and we're all going to be grateful."

Now her parents were speaking to Dr. Stone about Wat. How long had they been gone? Looking for the clock, Maxine glanced up at the wall-mounted television. Phil Donahue was interviewing a famous actress. Though Maxine couldn't hear what the actress was saying, she could see the people in the studio audience stand up and applaud. Phil applauded politely, as well. The actress said something else, something long, with a lot of hand gestures. Again, the studio audience rose and applauded.

It seemed so easy. You sat down next to Phil. You said what was on your mind. People applauded.

"C'mon, Maxie," her father called, walking back into the waiting room. He was smiling broadly. "C'mon, Wat. We're going home."

"Everything looked good," her mother called to Maxine, reading her thoughts. "Dr. Stone said Wat's heart was looking pretty handsome. He said he'll see us again in another six months."

"Can I come again?" she asked, giddy with relief.

"Sure," her father said, "you really kept him calm."

"You were great, Maxine," her mother added. "You should be a doctor when you grow up."

"But, I don't want . . ."

"Oh," her mother added, smiling. "Dr. Stone sends his best. He still remembers that time you snuck in to see him."

"C'mon, Wat," Maxine said, walking over to the blocks corner.

"Watch out!" Wat warned some imaginary demon lurking within his castle. "Prince Wat to the rescue!" He swept a small toy knight, his sword raised, over the castle's turrets.

Suddenly, Maxine felt a queer, cool flutter trickle down her back. It was that crazy idea that someday they would still have to give him back.

"Wat, who's in the castle?" she asked.

"The invisible dragon," he said, standing up and taking her hand.

"You're going to let him stay in there?" she asked, leading him toward her parents. "What if some poor kid sits next to it and the invisible dragon leaps out and eats him?"

"Too bad," Wat said. "He was there when I came in."

While her parents paid the cashier, Maxine helped Wat on with his baseball jacket. Again, she glanced up at the television. The actress was still speaking. It looked as if Phil were still interested in whatever she was talking about. So was the audience. When she was finished speaking, they applauded.

"Oh, Maxie," her mother said, laughing. "Dr. Stone wanted to know if you had come up with any new inventions lately."

"What did you tell him?" she asked.

"I told him fortunately not," she laughed. "He said he was disappointed."

Maxine looked up to Phil Donahue. She imagined herself on his show, leaning back in one of those black leather swivel chairs, waving her arms, and discussing her latest invention. Holding Wat's hand, pretending to listen to his story about the invisible dragon, she daydreamed all the way to the car, picturing herself as Phil's guest. She imagined the kids from her old school coming home, turning on their sets, and watching her explain how her new device worked. Boy, would they feel stupid, having spent all that time teasing her. "You're so boring," a girl had taunted her. "Why don't you invent yourself?" She pictured her parents seated in Phil's studio audience. After she spoke, they'd be forced to stand up and applaud with everybody else.

It seemed so easy. She just had to contact Phil.

Maxine Candle
34-37 59th Drive
Woodside, Queens
New York, NY 11377

August 20

Phil Donahue
NBC
30 Rockefeller Center
New York, NY 10112

Dear Phil,
   I think your time is running out. You need
to have me on your show. I'm almost an inventor, and you can make me famous. You
can ask me questions about my inventions.
You can get some people to start taking me
seriously.
   My mother doesn't. Wat, my little brother,
has a heart problem, and anytime I invent
something for him, my mother tells me I
worry too much.
   My father just thinks everything I do is
funny. He thinks I might be gifted and keeps
on trying to find out what I'm gifted in. Last
week he handed me a saxophone and told me
to blow. I made a horrible sound. A half hour
later, a bird flew into our window and died. I
don't think it was a coincidence.

Phil, I think your studio audience will like me. I'm almost nice to look at. I'm short, with brown curly hair. I wear glasses. I'm just a little pudgy, but I can dress nicely, and I can tell amusing stories about my family and my inventions.

I could tell about the time I was trying to change the tune on my mother's music box. I took it apart to see how it worked, but I got too close and my bottom lip got caught in the turning gears. While my lip was stuck, the little ballerina on the top kept twirling, smacking my nose with her hand. My father had to take me to the emergency room.

Phil, have me on your show. Make me famous. I'll bring all my invention ideas. You can talk to me like I was a real inventor.

Because someday, Phil, my brother might need a famous inventor to help fix his heart, and I want to be her.

Sincerely,

*Maxine Candle*

# ☆ 3 ☆

# Almost Famous

### *August 20*

M axine was having problems getting ready for fame. First, there was the problem of where she lived: Woodside, Queens. It wasn't the sort of place interesting people came from. There were no woods in Woodside. It was all tiny, narrow, identical two-family houses, one after another after another. On the top of the block was a potato-chip factory. On the bottom of the block was a car dealership. Her backyard was the size of a parking space, and on either side, her neighbors had put up ten-foot fences with curled barbed wire. Surrounded by those tall fences, she felt like a prisoner.

Her second problem was Wat. He wouldn't put on his tie. He was cranky. The bus had just brought him home from his last day at camp, and he had wanted to tell Maxine about his adventure. He didn't want to play talk show in the living room. He didn't want to pretend the banana was a microphone. He didn't want to wander into the imaginary studio audience and take questions for Maxine.

"We were in Alley Pond Park, and we followed a horse, and we got lost," Wat said. "Me and Letitia."

"First, ask me what my early years were like," Maxine suggested, trying to loop her father's tie over Wat's head.

"Debbie took us to find leaves, but we found a horse, and there was a policeman on top of him, and he had a gun," Wat said, trying to wriggle free.

"Stop squirming," Maxine insisted, trying to force the tie down over Wat's messy blond hair and large ears. "If I'm going to be on Phil's show, I'm going to need practice being famous. Ask me who my major influences were."

"No!" Wat shouted, pushing her away. He jerked the tie off his head and threw it onto the floor. "I don't want to play talk show! I'm only five! I got lost in the park, and the policeman had a gun, and Debbie yelled at me, and I didn't even get to bring back a ginkgo leaf."

"Wat, you like the inventions I make for you, right?" Maxine asked.

"No," Wat answered, shaking his head.

"Well, that's because they don't work, but if they worked, you'd like them, right?"

Wat was undecided.

"If I get to be famous, all my inventions will work," Maxine explained.

"The policeman let me give the horse a piece of sugar," Wat said. "His name was Breeze."

"The policeman's name was Breeze?" Maxine asked.

"No, the horse's name was Breeze," Wat answered. "The policeman had a gun. He didn't need a name."

"Wat," Maxine said, undoing the knot in her father's tie, "they're never going to let me be famous, unless I'm good at it. I need to practice. Here," she said, offering Wat the banana. "Just take some phone calls from our viewers at home."

"I want you to tell me a made-up story, Maxie," Wat said. "About an owl and a mouse, and the mouse wants to be a prince. Then I want to take a nap."

"You didn't take a nap at camp?" she asked.

"I got scared when they made us put our heads down."

"Why?" Maxine asked.

"Because I got scared," Wat said, sounding upset.

Accepting defeat, Maxine took Wat's hand and walked him to their bedroom. The room was divided in half by a folding screen. On Maxine's side of the screen were drawings for her inventions and pictures of her favorite inventors with their creations: Edison with his light bulb, Franklin with his lightning rod, and Bell with his telephone.

On Wat's side of the divider were horrifying pictures of dinosaurs attacking other dinosaurs, along with postcards from the Metropolitan Museum of Art of knights in armor. Maxine sat at the foot of Wat's bed.

"A made-up story about an owl and a mouse who wants to be a prince?" she asked.

"Yes," Wat said, looking under his bed for his stuffed walrus, Sir Walter.

Maxine closed her eyes and tried to picture the story. She had to see it first before she could tell it. That was the way she created all of her made-up stories. Concentrating, she began to see a mouse scampering back into his burrow, with a gum wrapper for a cape. But he would need a crown, she told herself. The owl would offer him a bottle cap, if only the mouse would come out of his burrow again. Just so the owl could measure his head.

Finding Sir Walter, Wat climbed up onto his bed. He leaned his head against Maxine's shoulder.

"It has to be a made-up story," he said, holding on tightly to Sir Walter.

"Once there was a proud mouse," Maxine began, "who lived all by himself. The forest floor was soft and dark, and all the mice lived by their own rules. The proud mouse thought, If only I was the prince of all mice. The owl was hungry . . ."

Wat was asleep. Gently inching away, Maxine let him slide off her shoulder and onto his pillow. She would let him sleep. Wat was having trouble sleeping lately at day camp. His counselors had informed their parents that he wouldn't nap in the daytime anymore. And at night, he was waking up with bad dreams.

It's these killer dinosaurs, Maxine thought, looking at Wat's pterodactyl clock. It was a quarter to five. Her father would be home in about fifteen minutes. She thought she had time. She could make some phone calls.

She knew she was crazy thinking Phil would have her on his show, just like that, just because she had written him a letter. Phil only had people on his show who were already famous. Leaving the bedroom for the kitchen, Maxine realized she would be a lot more interesting to Phil if he learned that she was the child of parents who were famous. Her father was a musician. He played at weddings and bar mitzvahs all over the area, even in New Jersey. Hundreds of people, maybe thousands of people, had seen him.

Flipping through her father's calendar attached to the refrigerator, Maxine looked for his next big engagement. It was for this Saturday. Quickly she called information and got the phone number of ABC News. She dialed the number.

"Hello, ABC News," a woman answered.

"Hello, ABC," Maxine said, trying to sound grown up and businesslike. "Who is your entertainment editor?"

"Larry Jackson," the woman said.

"Oh, Larry!" Maxine said. "Of course. Let me speak with him, please."

"Who is calling, please?"

"Just tell him it's me, Maxine."

After a click and a pause, the woman said, "I'm sorry, Maxine, Mr. Jackson isn't available now. Can I take a message?"

"Yes," Maxine said, trying not to sound too excited. "Tell him that William Candle's Jazz Quintet is playing a big gig this Saturday night. Why don't you get a crew there to film it? People are saying this William Candle is something special. The next Duke Ellington, maybe."

After a long pause the woman asked, "And where will Mr. Candle's Jazz Quintet be performing this Saturday?"

"At the Martinez wedding," Maxine read off the calendar. "At the V.F.W. Hall on Queens Boulevard."

"At the V.F.W. Hall on Queens Boulevard?" the woman repeated. "Hold on a second, please."

"Sure," Maxine said, trying to stay calm. She waited for the woman to return. "This is it!" she told herself. "Dad's going to be famous. I'm going to be the daughter of a famous person!"

"I'm sorry," the woman said, returning to the phone. "But apparently the crew is going to be covering the Pavarotti performance at the Metropolitan Opera House."

"But Pavarotti's already famous!" Maxine argued.

"I'm afraid you're right," the woman said.

"What about Sunday?" Maxine asked, quickly finding another mark on the calendar. "He's going to be playing the Goldstein bar mitzvah at the Great Neck Jewish Center."

"When is he going to be playing the Metropolitan Opera House?" the woman asked, sounding amused.

"When he's famous!" Maxine shouted into the phone.

She hung up, called information again, and got the number of CBS. She asked to speak to somebody from "60 Minutes." When they put her through, she told the man on the other end to send a crew over to her house on any Wednesday to film her father. "That's when he teaches Sean Xiu," she explained. "Sean's amazing. My father taught him how to play a whole song on the flügelhorn without making any mistakes."

"A whole song?" 60 Minutes asked.

"Yup!" Maxine admitted proudly. She liked "60 Minutes's" attitude. They sounded eager. "It's true. Just send somebody nice. Hello? Hello? . . . Hello?"

She tried NBC. NBC wasn't interested. They were polite. They asked her how old she was. They asked if she liked her school and her teacher. But they weren't interested in making her father famous.

"Maxine!" Her father was home. "Maxie, you got a package in the mail," he said, walking into the kitchen. "You didn't see it?"

"No," Maxine said, tearing open the large brown envelope and removing a booklet. On top of the booklet was a short note.

Dear Maxine the Inventor,
Thinking of you.

Best wishes,

There was no signature. The bottom of the note had been ripped when she had opened the envelope. Maxine read the title of the booklet: "The Inventions of Children Contest."

She opened it and looked inside.

"Prizes," it said, and underneath:

"1st place: $1,000, a trip to the Patent and Trademark offices in Washington, D.C., to meet with the Secretary of Labor, and an appearance on national television." She turned the page. "Entering the contest," it said. "Rules and regulations."

"What is it?" her father asked.

"The rules and regulations," she said, looking up at her father. He was a short man, with round glasses and a nose that had been broken when he tried to stop a fight between a tuba player and a drummer. He was nearly bald. He didn't look famous.

"Rules for what?" her father asked.

"Phil sent me a package," Maxine said, more to herself than her father.

"Phil who?" her father asked.

"Phil Donahue," she said, trying to convince herself. "He sent me the rules to the Inventions of Children Contest." She opened up the booklet again. "If I win it, he's going to have me on his show."

"Phil Donahue?" her father asked, grinning. He thought she was being funny.

"I wrote to him. He knows about me," Maxine informed him, and taking the booklet, she quickly walked back into her room.

Sitting down on her bed, she read that the deadline for entering the contest was October fifteenth. That wouldn't be any problem. She guessed she had millions of invention ideas. The fifteenth gave her plenty of time to develop one of them.

But then she read the first rule: "All entries must be submitted by a team of two inventors."

Now that was going to be a problem.

# ☆ 4 ☆

# A New Best Friend, Almost

## *September 9*

Standing at the entrance to P.S. 205's schoolyard at a few minutes before eight, Maxine held Wat's hand and looked for somebody to become her best friend for the rest of her life. It was a sunny, warm day, and kids were running all about the yard, climbing over the monkey bars, jumping rope, playing "steal the bases."

"Somebody here," she told Wat, "is going to become very important to my early years."

"Who?" Wat asked, leaning forward from the weight of his tyrannosaurus backpack.

"I don't know yet. I just feel it. Besides, that's the way it happens to all inventors before they become famous. They meet the right person," she explained, watching two little boys wrestling in the sandbox. "Bell met Ellis. Ellis showed him how you could use electricity to vibrate a tuning fork. Bell used that to invent the telephone."

"I thought you said you invented the telephone," Wat said.

"No, I told you I should have invented it," Maxine explained. "Bell invented it first. But only because he met Ellis. You have to meet the right person, Wat. Everybody met the right people at the right time. Shawlow met Townes and came up with the idea for the laser. And Judson met Earle."

"Who's Judson?" Wat asked.

"He invented the zipper. I could have invented that, too. You just have to meet the right person. I don't know," she said, smiling, "I'm feeling almost likable."

Wat looked puzzled.

"Maybe somebody will want to be my friend."

He still looked confused.

"Somebody has to be my friend," she explained. "The Inventions of Children Contest rules say you have to have a partner to enter the contest."

"Maxine," Wat asked, watching a yellow school bus pull up in front of the building, "do you think I'm going to have to nap during nap time?"

The doors of the bus opened. Instantly children began to stream onto the sidewalk, screaming and pushing past Maxine and Wat into the yard.

Maxine studied each kid who ran past her. She waited for one of them to stop, to notice she was new, to ask her who she was, did she have any hobbies?

"Inventing," she was prepared to say. "Inventing."

Nobody stopped. The children ran past her, unaware that there was anything special about her. Phil had written to her. She was almost famous. How could she still look like anybody else?

"Maxine," Wat said, tugging on her sleeve, "do you think they're going to make me take a nap?"

"What are you so worried about napping for?" she asked, searching the schoolyard for the right girl. What does an inventor look like? Taking Wat's hand, she led him into the yard.

"What if I don't want to?" he asked. "What if the teacher says I have to?"

"To nap?" Maxine asked.

Wat nodded.

"Listen, Wat, just put your head down, close your eyes, and drool," she suggested. "Nobody will know you're faking it."

"What if I pretend, and by accident I nap?"

"So?"

"I get bad dreams, Maxine."

"Wat, I'm in the building. Nothing's going to happen to you," she assured him. "I can get a pass and come down to your room in ten seconds."

To Maxine's right, a boy hung upside down on the monkey bars. His face began to redden and swell.

"But I get bad dreams," Wat said.

"I'll come down in two seconds," she promised.

"I'm not napping," Wat said conclusively.

Maxine watched the dangling boy's eyes begin to

bulge. His head was going to explode. She turned away. Two girls her own age raced past her, chasing a boy swinging a book bag.

"I wonder where she is?" Maxine asked.

Children were scattered all over the yard. Some boys played punchball. A few girls toward the back of the yard jumped Double Dutch. Boys Wat's age screamed as they tumbled over each other on the mats beneath the swings. Everywhere kids were playing or clustered in small groups, chatting and laughing. Everybody seemed to be with somebody else. Everybody was where they belonged. Nobody seemed to need her. But they didn't know, she was going to make them famous.

"There! Wat, there she is!"

Sitting alone in the back of the yard on a bench in the shade was a girl Maxine's age. She was drawing something on a pad. The way her long legs folded under the bench and her lanky arms held the pad reminded Maxine of a praying mantis. A few feet in front of the girl, in the sunlight, were five girls, standing in a line and practicing dance steps.

"Look, Wat." Maxine pointed out the girl. "She doesn't even notice those girls. I bet you she's inventing."

"I'm not napping," Wat reminded her.

"Wat! Look! That's her."

"How come she's sitting by herself?" Wat asked. "How come she's not dancing with those girls?"

"See"—Maxine knelt and pointed to the girl as if she were a rare bird—"she's keeping the problem constantly before her mind."

"What problem?"

"Let's go ask her," Maxine said, standing. She took Wat's hand.

Wat refused to move. "I don't want to talk to her."

"Why?" she asked.

"Because she doesn't look happy," he said.

The girl on the bench ripped out a piece of paper from her pad, crumpled it, and stuffed it into her pocket. She looked up and stared at the five girls in front of her practicing their dance steps. They clapped twice and spun around.

Maxine looked around to see if there was anybody else. Maybe she had missed somebody. Wat was right. The girl on the bench didn't look happy. Nobody else in the yard sat alone. All the other kids were in pairs or groups. Maybe something was wrong with her.

No, Maxine was sure, the girl was doing what Dr. Stone had said inventors do—keeping the idea constantly before her mind. She *had* to be an inventor. Nothing else mattered to her. That was it. An inventor had to think about her inventions. Even Maxine's own parents never seemed to understand that. How could she remember to pick up the eggs or put the detergent in the laundry? She had inventions on her mind. The kids at her old school never understood, either. She didn't have time to play silly girl games. She needed to think. She talked invention, they walked away. Or they teased her. Sometimes she wondered if an inventor was supposed to have friends. This girl on the bench was an inventor.

"C'mon, Wat." She grabbed his thumb and pulled him along. "You have the camera?"

"Yes," Wat said, sounding unhappy.

"It's too bad you didn't learn to write in that Happy Time nursery school," she complained.

Again Wat planted his feet. "I can make an *a* and a *t*, and I can make two *w*'s," he said proudly. "Big *W* and little *w*."

"Listen, Wat," Maxine said, resting her hands on his shoulders. "There are not very many interesting words you can make with an *a* and a big *W*, a little *w*, and a small *t*. I want you to promise me that the minute you learn at least two more vowels, you'll tell me."

"Why?"

"Because then you can start taking some notes about my inventions and my early life before I was famous."

"But I don't want to do that. I just want to learn how to read about dinosaurs and bugs, and good knights and bad knights, and . . . and . . . and I don't want to nap!"

"Come," Maxine insisted, and led him to the back of the yard to meet her new best friend.

The closer Maxine got, the less her new friend looked like a best friend. Sitting on that bench in the shade, her knees were pulled up against her chest as if she was trying to fit into some invisible box. Her hair was red, cut too short. Her bangs were messy. She had a long, bony face, sprinkled with freckles. She was wearing thick, round red glasses. Maxine slowed.

Wat squeezed her hand.

"Hey," Maxine called cheerfully, "what are you working on?"

"Being alone," the girl answered, not bothering to look up from her pad. "Now bug off."

Maxine stepped backward. She looked around. Maybe she had missed somebody, some girl her own age, some pretty girl, also working on her notepad. Someone friendly. Some girl who was just waiting for Maxine to show up with all her ideas. Her future best friend. She looked.

The dancing girls dropped to their knees, shook their heads, and clapped.

"Tell that boy!" they sang in unison.

She took another tentative step toward the girl. "Working on an invention?" she asked.

The girl looked up from her work. She tilted her head and glared at Maxine. Her mouth was a thin red line. "How did you know that?" she snapped.

"See!" Maxine told Wat. "I was right!"

"Who told you to come over here?" the girl asked, standing with her hands on her hips. She glared down at Maxine. "Alexander tell you to come here?"

"Who?"

"Alexander!" she repeated, as if Maxine were a fool.

"Who's Alexander?" Maxine asked. "I don't know who you're talking about. Do I?"

"Mr. Alexander," the girl said, studying Maxine, "the principal. He was just here, checking up on me as usual. I told him about the Inventions of Children Contest. My grandmother found out about it at church."

"I found out about it from Phil Donahue," Maxine said proudly. "He sent me the application."

"Did . . . did Michelle and Tammy tell you to come over here?"

Maxine shook her head. "No."

"Because I don't care what they think anymore. I'm not speaking to them anymore. I don't care what they call me. I'm not doing last year all over again. Let them get themselves into trouble."

"So what's your name?" Maxine asked, ignoring the girl's anger.

"Why?"

Maxine smiled, delighted by her luck. The girl backed away and then sat down. Maxine sat next to her new best friend. She had found her mirror image. It was too good to be true. She removed a pencil and a pad from her backpack. If she was going to be famous, she would need to begin putting together material for her biographers. Every inventor had a biographer. And she needed funny little stories to tell on Phil's show, something to amuse his studio audience. Speaking softly to herself, she wrote, "At first, my new best friend seemed angry and unfriendly. She wouldn't even tell me her name."

Maxine looked up and waited. The girl studied her face as if a foreign language were written across it.

Maxine returned to her notes. Continuing to speak out loud, she wrote, "But then she told me her name was—"

"Toni," the girl said warily.

Maxine filled in the blank. She looked up at Toni and smiled.

Toni quickly turned away to watch the girls practicing their dance steps.

In unison, the girls shook their hips, snapped their fingers, and slowly turned around.

"So go on home!" they sang.

"They think they're so perfect," Toni told Maxine, pointing to the girls, "and all of their mothers were born in heaven. I tell you, they deserve their mothers."

Maxine nodded.

"They're like five bodies with one head," Toni continued.

Maxine turned to Wat and caught him slowly backing away. "Where are you going?" she asked him. "C'mon, take out the camera."

Scrunching up his face, Wat collapsed onto the pavement and began to unzip his backpack. He muttered to himself.

"What is he doing?" Toni asked, standing.

Maxine also stood up. "I'm Maxine, and this is my brother, Wat. He's going to take our picture." She offered Toni her hand.

"He's going to do what?"

"Take our picture," Maxine cheerfully repeated, her hand dangling in the air.

"And why is he going to do that?" Toni asked, eyeing Wat suspiciously.

He had already removed his box of crayons and bag lunch. With his feet spread out in front of him, Wat struggled and pulled on the camera's strap. It was stuck inside his pack.

"Since we're going to be famous," Maxine explained to Toni, "I figured we should document our first meeting. You know, for posterity."

"What are you talking about?" Toni asked.

"For our biographies. For Phil's show."

Toni took a step toward Wat. Confused, she turned back to Maxine. She ran her thin fingers through her hair. She rested her hands on her hips. Tufts of red hair stuck up on her head. Toni's watery blue eyes were magnified by her thick glasses.

"So, what kind of invention are you working on?" Maxine asked.

"It's for my grand—" she started to say, then stopped. She hugged her chest and stared at Wat.

With the heels of his sneakers holding down his backpack, Wat continued to tug on the camera's strap. It didn't move. Muttering angrily to himself, he got onto his knees, crawled into the backpack, and began to operate on whatever was tangled. Crawling back out, he removed a bulky Polaroid. He stepped backward and peered into the viewfinder.

"Tell him to put that thing back into his bag," Toni said, softly but firmly. She tapped her foot.

Still peering into the viewfinder, Wat took another step backward.

Maxine smiled and returned to her notepad. "At first," she said aloud as she wrote, "Toni was not eager to have a picture taken."

"Will you stop that?" Toni asked. "Stop writing about me." She put her hands back on her hips. "Stop it."

Wat stopped retreating. He checked the picture counter, then looked back into the viewfinder.

"Hey, put that down!"

Wat lowered the camera and looked to Maxine.

"I said to put that thing away," Toni demanded. "Back into that pack, now, or I'm going to smash it. I didn't ask you to come here and get into my business," she told Maxine, pointing her finger at her nose. She turned to Wat. "Put it away. Now."

Frightened, Wat held on to the camera and waited for Maxine.

"He can't," Maxine explained.

"Why not?" Toni asked.

"It's his job."

"What?"

"That's his job. Since he always wants to follow me, I gave him a job. I thought he could help document my life before I became famous."

Toni stared at her in disbelief.

"You know and I know," Maxine said, "that nobody's going to take our inventions seriously unless we're famous."

"I want you to go away," Toni said calmly.

"Toni," Maxine assured her, "we're entering the contest as partners. You'll be famous too."

"Stop saying that," Toni insisted, stamping her foot. "Why do you keep saying that?"

"Because Phil Donahue wrote me a letter. He sent me the application for the Inventions of Children Contest."

"Yeah, right."

"He did," Maxine said firmly. "I've been inventing things since I was five. He probably figured it was about time I was on his show. So he sent me the rules of the contest. You read the rules?"

"Yes."

"The first rule says each invention has to be submitted by a team of two inventors. That's why I came looking for you. I knew you'd be here."

"You don't even know me."

"But I knew you'd be here," Maxine insisted. "I knew it."

"You know what else you should know?" Toni asked, almost smiling. "You're a crazy person."

"No, I'm not," Maxine said defensively.

"Yes, you are," Toni assured her. "You come around taking people's pictures and writing about them when you don't even know them. That's not normal."

"I just figured you were going to be my . . . It made sense. It always happens that way. In my book *Great Inventors* it said that—"

"Listen," Toni said, holding up her hand and waving Maxine away. "You just stay away from me. Far away."

"What about the contest?"

"You just think," Toni said, turning her back to Maxine and angrily stuffing her notepad into her backpack, "you just want something, it happens. Like you deserve it. Like only nice things should happen to you. Like the angels in heaven are sitting there, waiting for your prayers." She turned to face Maxine. "Who sent you over here and told you about me?"

"Nobody," Maxine insisted. "I don't even know anybody in the school. This is my first day. I was just looking for my future best friend. I need a partner."

"So you picked me?" Toni shook her head in disbelief.

"You looked like an inventor."

"Go away."

"What class are you in?" Maxine asked.

"Mr. Seligman's class, 5-401."

"You're in my class!"

"I said, go away."

"Wat! Get the camera!" Maxine shouted. Quickly she picked up her pencil and began to write and say aloud, "By coincidence, Toni and I were put into the same class. Though she didn't know it at the time—"

"Stop that!"

Maxine glanced over at Wat. He was clumsily trying to pop up the flash attachment. They were in the shade.

"Listen to me," Toni advised Maxine. "Don't talk to me when we get into class. I'm not talking to anybody this year."

"What about the contest? The rules say—"

"I don't care what the rules say. I don't need a partner. I'm going to enter it by myself. I'll make up a partner. I've been thinking about it all summer. I promised my grandmother I was going to do something for her this year. I told her I was going to make up for last year. She doesn't even believe me. It's all I've been thinking about. Don't mess it up."

"Wat!"

"What?"

Pop!

Maxine staggered backward, her hands over her eyes.

"Sorry," Wat called. "I pressed the button. It was an accident."

Trying to erase the purple dots that floated in front of her, Maxine rubbed her eyes and squinted. Toni was gone. Wat handed Maxine the camera.

"Not a good photo opportunity, Wat," she said, as they watched the picture develop together.

> Maxine Candle
> 34-37 59th Drive
> Woodside, Queens
> New York, NY 11377
>
> September 10

Phil Donahue
NBC
30 Rockefeller Center
New York, NY 10112

Dear Phil,

I think you should have a show called "Children Who Are Almost Famous Inventors." I could be on your expert panel. I could tell your viewers about my first day of school.

When I walked into Mr. Seligman's class for the first time, I introduced myself. I told him I already had a few ideas for the contest.

He suggested I take a seat.

I informed him that I was almost famous.

He told me I could take any seat I wanted.

Just to let him know who I was, that I wasn't some silly little kid, I told him about some of my inventions and mentioned how I was working on a chalk that sparkles.

He said that was "nice," but still didn't look at me. He wouldn't let go of the chalk runners and he wouldn't take his eyes off that door. I couldn't help wondering who he was waiting for.

I took the booklet for the Inventions of Children Contest out of my bag and read him the second rule, which says that the inventor's teacher must follow the contest's guidelines and provide the winning team with a written statement of support.

I pointed out that he was *that* teacher.

He wasn't interested.

Now *I* began to get nervous. I needed him. According to the rules, if your teacher doesn't help you, you can't compete.

"You're a new teacher?" I asked him. "You ever teach before?"

He shook his head.

I figured I needed to impress him, to make him know I was talking about important matters, and I was for real. I offered to let him try my sparkle chalk.

He said he didn't need a chalk that sparkles.

"Why not?" I asked him. I told him I hadn't tried it yet, but it would make everybody pay attention, and I didn't think it would explode.

He wasn't interested.

I pointed out to him that his board was empty, he was a new teacher, and it would be such a wonderfully dramatic way to start off the year.

He walked away from me and closed the door. Everybody had come in.

Phil, right now Mr. Seligman is trying to get the class's attention. The girl to my left is doing her nails. The boy to my right is reading some kind of magazine about soldiers. Mr. Seligman is rapping his knuckles against his desk, trying to get anybody to look up at him. A boy in the back, I just noticed, is wearing headphones. Toni, my invention partner, is sitting with her chair facing the window.

Phil, it does not look good in here. What do I do? The air is not filled with the sparks of creativity. I am beginning to feel more and more almost, and less and less, famous.

Sincerely yours,

*Maxine Candle*

## ☆ 5 ☆

# Paparazzo

### September 13

**"M**axine," her father said, entering the kitchen, "why is Wat standing out in the backyard with your camera?"

"Oh, is he?" Maxine asked. She casually glanced behind her. "Look at that," she said to herself. She shrugged and returned to her drawing. "Kids."

"Didn't notice him before, did you?" her father said. He laughed softly.

"I'm working on an invention. I've been lost in thought." She glanced up at her father to see if he believed her.

His eyebrows were raised. He laughed again and shook his head, put his sheet music down on the table, and opened the refrigerator door. He removed a container of milk. "What is Wat standing on?" he asked.

"A milk crate, but don't pay any attention to him." She returned to her drawing. She was trying to design a hamster-driven pencil sharpener. She needed to in-

vent something that would convince Mr. Seligman and
Toni she was for real. Attached to the axis of the
hamster's wheel, the sharpener would turn as the
hamster exercised, littering the bottom of its cage with
shavings and providing sharp pencils to its owner.

"How did the milk crate get there?"

"Dad," she asked, looking up from her drawing,
"where do hamsters run wild?"

"That's a very good question, Maxine," her father
said, bringing a glass of milk and some cookies to
the table. "But I have a better one. Why is Wat
standing on a milk crate outside, trying to take your
picture?"

"That is a good question, Dad," Maxine acknowl-
edged. "But I have a better one. I was just wondering,
Where would you be if you suddenly came across a
pack of hamsters in their natural habitat?"

"Maxine . . ."

"And why do they need wheels? Do they have
wheels in the wild? Are there some sort of natural
wheels that hamsters run on?"

"Maxine, how did the milk crate get there? Let's
start with that one," her father said, sitting down opposite her. He opened his book of sheet music.

"He asked me to put it there."

"All right. Here we go. And why did he do that?"

"He said he wanted to play paparazzo."

"Paparazzo. Those were his words?"

"Not exactly," she admitted, turning around to

watch Wat struggle to keep his chin above the kitchen
window. His nose was pressed against the glass.
He held the camera high above his head, as if he
were sinking and trying to keep it dry. He didn't look
happy.

"Maxine . . ."

"He wanted to play that game where you pretend
you're a photographer sneaking around, trying to get
a photo of a famous person at home, doing something
natural, like snacking on milk and cookies and working
on an invention."

"He did?" her father asked. "He went up to you and
said, 'Maxie, I want to play that game in which I run
around outside the house with your camera and try to
sneak pictures of you so I can sell them to supermar-
ket tabloids like the *Enquirer* and the *Star* and *People*
magazine.' That's what he asked you?"

"Those weren't his exact words," she admitted.

"And you agreed to play the famous person?" her
father guessed.

"Yes."

"Why does he do it, Maxie?" her father asked, waving hello to her brother. Wat waved back. Then he
disappeared. Her father stood up. He took a quick step
toward the kitchen door. Suddenly the camera reap-
peared, followed by the top of Wat's head. Her father
sighed, and cautiously returned to his chair. "Your
mother and I are always amazed at what he lets you
do to him."

"I don't do anything to him," Maxine said defensively.

"Sure you do," he said, amused. "You experiment on him!"

"Well, who else am I going to experiment on?" she asked. "If I invent something for him, I have to test it to see if it works. Maybe he follows me around because he's waiting for me to invent something for him someday. Maybe ..." Suddenly she started to feel shaky, frightened. "Maybe he thinks I'll invent something to fix his heart."

"Maxine," her father said, reaching across the table and taking her hand. "Look at me. Nobody is waiting for you to fix Wat's heart."

"But what if someday he needs to have his heart fixed? What if nobody's invented something to fix it? What then?"

"Maxine, don't worry about it," her father insisted. "You are just a little girl."

"But if I become an inventor now, a famous inventor, I bet I could invent something ..."

"Maxine, your brother is going to be fine."

"If he's going to be fine, why do you keep taking him back to the doctor? Why do you keep taking him for tests? Why do you keep looking at his heart? Is something going to happen?"

"No. Nothing is going to happen."

"Wat's waiting for something to happen," she said, looking toward the back door. Again the camera was sinking below the windowpane. "I think he's scared. I think that's why he won't nap. I think he gets scared about his heart. Maybe he's waiting for me to invent something. Maybe that's why he follows me."

"What about friends?" her father asked. "For you, your own age."

"You don't want Wat to follow me?"

"I want Wat to look up to you. But I don't want him to follow you because he thinks you're going to invent something to fix his heart. I think sometimes your inventions . . ." Her father paused to think about what he was going to say. "Maybe you worrying about Wat makes him worry too much."

"But I want to be able to do something."

"I was thinking of you. Sticking to Wat so closely and working on your inventions makes it difficult to find good friends."

"I have a good friend," Maxine said defensively. "Her name is Toni. She's interested in inventing too. And she's a great artist. Today in Ms. Quick's class, Toni drew a building in charcoal. It almost looked like a photograph without color. I think it was her building. It was kind of sad looking, but Ms. Quick, the art teacher, held it up. She said she had never seen such 'expert use of shadowing.' She's my friend."

"Toni?" her father asked.

"Yes," Maxine said. "We became friends. Just like that."

"That's great, Maxie," her father said. "I'm glad to hear that. Sometimes your mother and I worry. We want you to have friends."

"Toni's my friend."

"Why don't you bring Toni over?"

"I will, I will. Look at the invention," she said, handing her father her drawing. "What do you think?"

Her father took off his glasses and studied the picture. Maxine thought about what she had left out of the story: how Toni had shrugged and looked away from the other kids to the window, how after Ms. Quick returned Toni's artwork to the Masterpieces Table and walked away, Toni grabbed the drawing, ripped it up, and shoved the pieces into her desk.

"You know," Maxine had said to Toni after class, "you draw like an almost-famous person."

"Don't talk to me again," Toni had answered her. "You make me want to hurt you."

"Now this is . . . interesting," Maxine's father said, holding up her drawing.

He doesn't know what he's looking at, Maxine told herself. If only she were a better artist. She took it back. Her hamster looked like a cigar with legs and teeth. Her sharpener didn't look like anything. She was a terrible artist. Ms. Quick hadn't even patted her on the back in art class. How was she going to win the contest if she couldn't make clear drawings? Rule number three of the contest stated, "All entries must be accompanied by accurate drawings of the invention, illustrating its function and purpose. Drawings should be suitable for publication."

"Where's your homework?" her father asked.

She didn't know what to say. She had forgotten to copy it down.

"You know, Maxine, next year is junior high school. If you don't get a good report card, if you get another card like last year's, it's going to be hard to get into a good school."

"You think if I was a famous inventor, it would be easy?"

"I think if you spend too much time inventing and too little time paying attention to your classwork and your homework, nothing's going to be easy."

"What do you think of my invention?" she asked, trying to change the subject. "It's a hamster sharpener."

"Now that's a clever idea," her father said, turning the drawing sideways. "The sharper the hamster, the easier it will be for him to open his seeds."

She took back her drawing. She stared at it. She had no partner for the contest. Her teacher wasn't interested. She couldn't draw well enough to be taken seriously. "It's for pencils, Dad," she said, exasperated. "The hamster turns the wheel and that turns the pencil sharpener."

"I was just kidding, Maxie." He smiled. "It's very . . . clever. But listen, Maxine, your mother and I have looked into the school situation. There's only one good junior high in the area, J.H.S. 44. They have a gifted and talented program. If you work hard this year, there's no reason you shouldn't get in."

"I *should* get in, because I'm gifted and talented."

"Well, how are they going to know that if you don't get a good report card?"

"They can turn on the 'Donahue' show." Maxine took her glass and walked over to the sink. "I'll clean up," she said, and turned on the hot water. Glancing out the back window, she saw two small hands and part of a camera, but no Wat. The camera was pointed at her empty seat. If he pressed the shutter now, she realized, she wouldn't even show up in the picture.

She had to do something soon, something to prove to Mr. Seligman, to her father, to Toni, that she wasn't just another normal, uninteresting, ungifted, and un-talented kid.

Washing her plate, she noticed two clear rubber gloves her mother used for doing the dishes. She had an idea.

"I'm going upstairs to listen to this," her father said, holding up his music. "When Sean comes with his flü-gelhorn, just send him upstairs."

"I won't be here," she said, taking his empty glass. "I have to go to the pet store. I'll be right back."

"What about your brother?" her father asked.

"He'll follow me," Maxine said, drying her hands. "That's what he does."

Maxine Candle
34-37 59th Drive
Woodside, Queens
New York, NY 11377

September 13

Phil Donahue
NBC
30 Rockefeller Center
New York, NY 10112

Dear Phil,

Even my best ideas are becoming useless.

Today, after waiting about twenty minutes for us to get settled—he still hasn't given out our permanent seats—Mr. Seligman asked, If we were going on a long boat ride to a new place, what would we bring?

I considered this a good question. It almost had something to do with inventing. I opened my notebook and began to jot down ideas. I also readied the Device. I invented it the night before. I figured it would help some people take me seriously.

When nobody said anything, Mr. Seligman told us to think like the Pilgrims. What would we bring to the New World if we were Pilgrims?

Victor, the boy to my right, said, "A gun."

Mr. Seligman thought that was a good idea, then asked why Victor would bring a gun.

"For food," Victor said.

Mr. Seligman asked him what sort of food.

"Eggs," Victor said.

Mr. Seligman looked a little confused. He asked Victor why he would need a gun for eggs.

"To shoot the chickens!" said Victor.

Phil, maybe you should have a show called "Children Who Should Never Be Famous." Victor could be on your expert panel.

Mr. Seligman looked around the classroom to call on somebody else.

Of course I had an idea. It had to do with a trap for turkeys. It used a cranberry mold as bait. But of course Mr. Seligman wasn't going to call on me. This is the only thing I have learned in school so far. I can raise my hand and raise my hand, but Mr. Seligman will only call on somebody who goes "Oooh! Oh! Ooh-oh-*oooh!*" and waves her hand like she's trying to clean the windows of a moving car.

So I brought out the Device.

I called it the Inflatable Hand. I had borrowed one of my mother's clear rubber gloves. I had bought thin rubber aquarium tubing at the pet store. I put the glove on my right hand and stuck the tube inside my palm into the glove. I ran the other end of the tube through my sleeve up to my shoulder, out of my collar into my mouth.

I began to blow.

Mr. Seligman called on somebody else, a girl who said she'd bring a fishing pole. Another kid said he'd bring seeds. Another said he'd bring a radio to listen to the weather.

Mr. Seligman reminded him we were talking about the Pilgrims, who lived a long time ago.

"So they didn't have weather?" the boy asked.

"No," Mr. Seligman explained. "They had weather, they just didn't have electricity."

My glove began to fill with air. Mr. Seligman continued, as usual, to ignore me. A girl in the back said she'd bring something to trade with the Indians. My glove began to swell. Bigger and bigger.

Mr. Seligman called on the kids who made the loudest "oohs" and "ahhhs." Victor suggested that if he didn't need his gun, he'd bring his eggs and plant them as soon as he arrived.

I continued to blow into the tube. My hand was becoming the size of Brazil. Finally Mr. Seligman called on me.

I forgot what I was going to say. I think it was because everybody was staring at my hand.

Mr. Seligman asked me what was wrong with my hand.

I stared at it. My hand belonged in the Macy's Thanksgiving Day Parade.

I said it was just allergies.

It looked diseased.

Then it exploded.

Then Isabel Montanez, who sits to my left and has three bottles of nail polish carefully arranged at the edge of her desk, fainted.

I never saw anybody faint in real life before.

Neither had Mr. Seligman.

This could be an interesting story to tell on your show: how Mr. Seligman handled such a medical emergency, and how, even though he hadn't assigned seats to anybody else, he moved my desk and my chair—with me still sitting in it!—to the very back of the class, right next to Toni.

Any suggestions?

Sincerely,

*Maxine Candle*

P.S. Toni, who still doesn't know she is going to become my best friend, just read this letter over my shoulder. She said I was really something, and I had some imagination. Then she told me not to go anywhere after school, to meet her on the steps. She warned me not to run away. She didn't want to go looking for me.

I said, "Sure."

Phil, I'm in the girls' room now, where I just finished writing this P.S. I'm going to sneak to the main office and mail this letter before I return to class. When you get it, keep it. If something should happen to me this afternoon, it could be used as evidence.

## ☆ 6 ☆

# Inventing Toni

### Later That Same Day

**"Y**ou know, I've been thinking about this meeting all afternoon, Toni," Maxine explained as the class made its way downstairs to the front door. "I think it's a bad idea. For many reasons. First, I really haven't done anything to offend you. Second, even though we really haven't started yet, it's going to hurt our friendship, and set us back in the Inventions of Children Contest. And third, it's going to hurt me. I don't know how to fight. I've never been in a fight before. You're much bigger than me." She shifted uneasily and looked up into Toni's sharp eyes. She stared at Toni's earrings: oversize gold hoops. "Your earrings," Maxine pointed out, "are much bigger than me. Almost."

They passed through the doors opening out onto the stairs that led down to the sidewalk. Stepping aside to avoid the kids rushing past her, Maxine searched the clusters of parents, aunts and uncles, and older brothers and sisters for help. The sunlight was strong, forcing her to squint and shade her eyes with her hand. Peering down into the crowd, she watched a small boy, about Wat's age, jump into the arms of his mother.

"Where's your brother?" Toni asked, her arms folded.

"He's in his after-school program. I don't remember if today is storytelling or judo."

"Good," Toni said, moving closer. She seemed to want to confide in Maxine. "You have any money?" she asked quietly.

Maxine looked down into the crowd for an adult without a child, somebody she could attach herself to, somebody she could cling to and follow home.

"Do you have any?" Toni repeated.

"No," Maxine lied.

"Not good," Toni said to herself. "Listen," she told Maxine. "Follow me and listen." She took Maxine by the arm and led her down the steps and up to the block along Thirty-ninth Avenue.

"I'm going to give you five dollars, and you're going to do me a favor. Is that all right?"

If I start running, Maxine thought, if I make it to the school, I can run through the crowd, up the block, and turn left. I can be home in two minutes.

"Well?" Toni asked, pausing, her arms folded across her chest. She looked as if she were hugging herself for warmth.

Maxine watched some children carry their books into the Woodside Library across the street. It was probably a safe place. As soon as the traffic stopped, she could sprint to it.

"Maxine," Toni said, tapping her foot. She took a deep breath and looking up the block asked, "You'll do it?"

"No," Maxine said curtly.

"What?"

"Just say no. I'm just saying no. No," Maxine quietly insisted. "No. You shouldn't be involved in that stuff."

"What stuff?" Toni asked, angry and confused.

"Drugs," Maxine mumbled. "They're nothing but bad news. Just say no."

"What are you talking about?"

"You're only ten years old," Maxine said. "You're a great artist. You can become a famous inventor. Why are you going to throw it all away—"

"Stop it."

"I'm saying no. No. No."

"I said stop it."

"No."

"Stop it!" Toni shouted, covering Maxine's mouth with her hand. "Stop talking. I want you to buy my grandmother flowers. Flowers!"

Toni released her grip. "Then I want you to come over to my house and talk like you always talk. I want you to pretend you're my friend in front of my grandmother."

"Flowers?"

"I can't go into the store and buy them myself. I can't go into most of the stores here. Last year I was hanging out with these kids, and we got caught trying to rip them off. I . . . used to do that kind of stuff."

"What kind of flowers?" Maxine asked.

"I don't know," Toni said, looking both worried and embarrassed. "I think she likes . . . what does your mother like?"

"Daisies?" Maxine guessed.

"Can you buy her daisies, then?" Toni asked eagerly. "You . . . if I give you money, you can keep the change."

"I don't want to do that," Maxine said.

Toni looked hurt.

"I don't want to keep the change. I'll buy the flowers. I just have to be back by four to pick up Wat."

Toni smiled, but then turned away from Maxine and began walking quickly along Thirty-ninth Avenue. "There's a place near my apartment," she called back.

Reaching Roosevelt Avenue, they walked into the shadows cast by the elevated-train tracks for the number seven line. On either side of the street were small shops with their lights on, as if it were night. Walking in and out of slats of light and shade, they passed bars, a stationery store, and Garcia's Botanica, with its religious statues in the window. The number seven train screeched above them. Maxine stuck her fingers in her ears. Her whole body shook from the vibrations of the train. They passed McReynold's Funeral Home.

"I wouldn't want to die here!" Maxine shouted. "It's so noisy!"

"Maybe it would wake you up!" Toni shouted back, laughing.

Above the shops were apartments, two and three
stories up, their windows closed to the noise of the
train. Somebody had painted a flower box with pink
and yellow flowers over one of the windows. Maxine
guessed nobody ever opened it. She also wondered if
the tracks were close enough to the windows that you
could jump from one to the other.

"How can people live like that?" she shouted to Toni.

"They're probably stuck!" Toni shouted back, turning left down Fifty-fifth Street. Leaving the shadows
of the train tracks, Maxine removed her fingers from
her ears. She followed Toni past the fenced-in yard of
Antonelli's Monuments, with its tombstones and a
statue of a stone woman, her arms outstretched, plead-
ing. Toni picked up the pace. They walked past ware-
houses, a boarded-up ice cream store; past an
abandoned house, its yard strewn with weeds. At Hector's Rent-a-Wreck, a Doberman leapt against its fence
and barked at Maxine. She jumped.

"Where are we going?" she asked.

"One more block," Toni said.

Again they walked into shadows as they passed under the train trestle of the Long Island Railroad.
Across the street, next to a row of battered, wooden
homes, was a small grocery store. One of its windows
was covered with a board. Cigarette and beer posters
covered its other windows. In front of the store, on
wooden tiers, were fruits and flowers. Suddenly the
ground began to shake. Maxine turned around and
looked up to see the steel webbing of the bridge begin

to sway. A train was coming. She put her fingers back into her ears and turned to the store to watch a young woman come out, pushing a stroller and drinking something out of a paper bag. She was wearing a dirty down coat buttoned up to her neck, though it was at least sixty degrees out. Looking more closely, Maxine noticed there wasn't any baby in the stroller.

Suddenly Maxine's whole body began to shake. Staring straight up, she watched the undercarriage of the train rumble toward Manhattan.

"That's it!" Toni shouted, pointing to the store.

Maxine pulled her fingers out of her ears. "Flowers?" she asked.

"Daisies!" Toni shouted. "Something pretty! Something your mother would like!"

"Does this mean," Maxine shouted as the train thundered above, "you'll be my partner in the contest?"

Toni laughed. After watching the last car lurch away, she turned back to Maxine. "Didn't anybody warn you to keep away from me?" she asked, searching through her pockets. "Wait, I think I have it." She pulled out two crumpled bills. "Damn!" she cursed, unfolding the money. "I thought I had five dollars. How much do you think they'll cost?"

"Why should I be warned?" Maxine asked Toni. "Why should I keep away from you?"

"If nobody told you, I won't," Toni said. "Here." She offered Maxine her money. "You think they'll cost more than two dollars?"

"Why should I be warned?"

"Why don't you get the flowers? We have to get you back to pick up your brother."

Taking the money, Maxine looked both ways, then ran across the street. Standing in a vase next to some mangoes and papayas was a bunch of daisies for three dollars. She grabbed them and ran inside. She started to cough. The store smelled of cigarette smoke and something sour. Its floors were powdered in sawdust. A ceiling-high plastic booth surrounded the counter. Digging into her pocket, she found a single dollar. Coughing and sneezing, she knocked on the booth. A fat bald man opened a small door.

"What you got?" the man growled.

"Daisies," she said nervously, as if she were doing something wrong, as if she were buying something illegal.

The man stuck his fat hand through the small door. She placed the three singles onto his palm and ran back out.

"They're pretty!" she called, crossing the street. She handed Toni the flowers. "My father's planning on growing them in our backyard."

Toni shook her head. "You always seem to know the wrong thing to say, don't you?" she asked.

"Your grandmother's going to like them," Maxine said, feeling hurt.

"How much did they cost?" Toni asked, sniffing the flowers.

"Daisies don't smell," Maxine informed her.

Toni looked up. "How much did they cost?"

"Two dollars," Maxine said.

"Don't be nice to me, Maxine," Toni warned her.

"They were on sale," Maxine insisted. "They're day-old flowers."

"Well, they're still pretty," Toni said, walking quickly in the direction of the train, again trying to smell the flowers. "You think she'll like them?"

"All grandmothers like daisies," Maxine said, nearly running to keep up with Toni.

"I'm on the next block."

The next block began with a vacant lot, fenced in, strewn with weeds, dirt mounds, and cinder blocks. In the middle of the lot, like a joke, was an overstuffed green couch and coffee table set opposite a television with its screen shattered. At the end of the lot was a three-story brick building. The building's front door was covered by a steel plate.

Reaching the building's stoop, Toni stopped and turned to face Maxine. She pointed the flowers at Maxine's nose. "I just want you to tell my grandmother"— she paused and took a deep breath—"I just want you to tell her how we're such good friends, and how well I'm doing in school."

"What's her name?"

"Mrs. Skye, but listen," Toni said, tucking the flowers under her arm and removing her keys. "Don't take out your pad and start writing down what she says. My grandmother doesn't want to be famous."

"You just want me to talk?" Maxine asked.

"I want you to tell her how we're best friends, and

we do Double Dutch, and tell her how we're working on the Inventions of Children Contest, and how Mr. Seligman thinks we're the best."

"You want me to make things up?" Maxine asked.

Toni didn't answer her. Turning the key, she rammed the door open with her hip, dug her hands into her pockets, and walked hurriedly across the narrow corridor to the stairs. After pushing the door closed with her shoulder, Maxine ran after Toni up three flights. Toni stopped in front of an apartment at the end of the hall.

"Grandma!" Toni called, opening the door.

The apartment was dark and quiet. Maxine stepped inside. It smelled of medicine. She glanced at her watch. It was already three-thirty. She had to get back to Wat by four.

"How are you, Grandma?" Toni asked, with forced cheer.

"Tired," her grandmother said flatly.

Dressed in a terry-cloth robe, she was sitting on an overstuffed couch in the dusty light by the window. Her face was thin and pale, her gray hair cut to her shoulders. She wore bifocals. She was holding open a thick book on her lap. None of the lights were on in the apartment.

"Hi." Maxine waved, taking a tentative step forward.

"Look what I brought you, Grandma," Toni said, holding up the daisies. "Flowers!"

"Daisies," Maxine added.

"I do like daisies," Mrs. Skye told Maxine. Her voice was thin and splintery.

"That's what Toni told me," Maxine said, making herself smile.

She watched Toni cautiously approach her grandmother, holding the flowers in front of her as if they were a peace offering. As Mrs. Skye took them, Toni sat down beside her and gave her a quick kiss on the cheek. She began to stroke her grandmother's hair.

Mrs. Skye reached behind her and pulled the cord on a standing lamp behind the couch. The bulb flashed, forcing Maxine to squint and rub her eyes. When she could see again, she noticed Toni's grandmother was staring at her.

"The flowers are pretty, aren't they?" Maxine asked.

"They are," Mrs. Skye said, closing her book. It was a Bible. She turned to Toni. "What are you doing bringing me flowers? Where did you get them? You steal them?"

"No," Toni said, "I didn't steal them from anywhere, Grandma. We—"

"We just bought them downstairs at the grocery store," Maxine interrupted. "Toni said . . . Toni said when she thinks of you, she thinks of daisies."

"And who are you?" Mrs. Skye asked.

"Maxine, I'm Maxine," she said, as if she were a long-lost relative. "I'm Maxine, Toni's new best friend. We do Double Dutch together. We study together. And we're partners in the Inventions of Children Contest. Here." She gently took the daisies away from Mrs. Skye and walked off toward the small kitchen. "Let me put these in water."

"Toni," Mrs. Skye asked, "who is this little girl?"

"She's my new friend, Grandma," Toni said, twining strands of her grandmother's hair. "And . . . and . . . she's almost famous."

"Stop talking such nonsense," Mrs. Skye protested.

"No, it's true, Grandma. She writes to Phil Donahue. She's going to be on his show."

"She's going to be on the 'Donahue' show. Why are you telling me stories? Who is she?"

"Grandma, it's true."

"Toni," Maxine called from the kitchen. There were no vases. The kitchen was narrow and smelled stale and damp, of old cigarettes and opened milk. She peered into the cabinet above the sink. There were a few cans of vegetables, Vienna sausages, and some smudged glasses. No vases. "Toni, where do you keep your vases?"

"We don't have any," Toni called back.

"Oh," Maxine said. She opened the refrigerator. Inside were two bruised bananas, some bologna, a few eggs, and two bottles of orange juice, one nearly empty. "I'm going to pour out this bottle," she said, holding it up. "It's almost empty anyway. I'll fill it with water for the flowers. All right?"

"How come she's here?" Mrs. Skye asked Toni. "You threaten her to come here?"

"No," Toni insisted.

"I can use the orange juice bottle?" Maxine asked again. "It's nearly empty."

"Yes!" Toni yelled. "Use it." She lowered her voice. "Grandma, she's my friend. She's nice."

"Toni," her grandmother said, "you know how tired I am. If—"

"Here you go!" Maxine sang, carrying the orange juice bottle with its daisies into the living room. Pushing aside some old newspapers on the coffee table, Maxine set the bottle down in front of Mrs. Skye. "Daisies!" she announced.

"Tell her," Toni urged Maxine. "Tell her about Phil Donahue."

"Well," Maxine said, sitting down on the other side of Mrs. Skye, "I haven't been on his show yet, but we're almost like friends already. He knows I'm an inventor. He sent me the rules for the Inventions of Children Contest so I could win and be on his show. He's like that. I write to him all the time."

"Phil Donahue," Mrs. Skye said doubtfully.

"Phil Donahue," Maxine repeated. "Toni's going to be on the show, too."

"Toni is going to be on 'Donahue' with you?"

"You need a partner to enter the Inventions of Children Contest," Maxine explained. "And Toni and I are going to be partners. Mr. Seligman already said"— Maxine looked across to Toni and smiled—"Toni's invention ideas are the best in the class. They're the best he's seen since he became a teacher."

Mrs. Skye looked doubtfully at Toni.

"That's what he said," Maxine insisted.

"He said that, Grandma, he did," Toni agreed.

"And . . . he's right," Maxine said. "I should know. I've been inventing things since I was a little kid, and even I think Toni's newest invention idea is brilliant."

"What invention?" Mrs. Skye asked her granddaughter.

"I know what I'm talking about, Mrs. Skye," Maxine assured her. "I mean, I could be considered an expert."

"What invention?" Mrs. Skye asked.

"Grandma, I was just thinking that I could make something to help you with your sleeping . . ."

"What are you talking about?" Mrs. Skye asked.

"Don't tell her," Maxine insisted. She took Mrs. Skye's hands and held them. "It's a secret. We can't talk about it until we're finished. Those are the rules."

"That's true, Grandma," Toni added. "If we told you, we'd be eliminated from the contest."

"That's the rule," Maxine echoed. "But let me just tell you one thing, Mrs. Skye. All Toni ever talks about is her invention. Mr. Seligman said he can't believe she's still doing so well in math and reading when she's spending so much time experimenting and planning with me."

"Since when did you become friends with my granddaughter?" Mrs. Skye asked, looking at Maxine suspiciously.

"Since the first day of school. As soon as we saw each other, we knew we were going to become best friends. That's the way it always happens to inventors right before they make their great discoveries. They meet the right people."

"She's not hanging around with those bad girls anymore?"

"No. Just with me. We're inseparable," Maxine boasted, looking over to Toni. "Right?"

"Right." Toni nodded.

"She's not getting herself in trouble anymore? No more fights?"

"She's too busy."

"She's not talking back to her teacher?"

"She's Mr. Seligman's favorite student," Maxine said. "He can't stop—"

"Grandma," Toni interrupted, "I've got to take Maxine back to school now. She's got to pick up her little brother."

"He's probably really tired by now," Maxine explained. "He won't nap during nap time."

"Maxine!" Toni urged.

"He took a picture of the two of us," Maxine continued, standing and shaking Mrs. Skye's hand. "Of our first encounter."

"Oh?"

"It shows us before we knew we were going to be best friends for life."

"I'll be right back, Grandma," Toni said, gently pulling Maxine's hand.

"Here." Mrs. Skye pushed herself up from the couch. She reached into a pocket of her robe and pulled out some single dollar bills. She offered them to Toni. "Pick up some dinner for yourself on the way back."

Toni glanced down at the money. She looked up at her grandmother. "What about you?"

"I'm not hungry," she said. "Just get yourself something." She turned to Maxine. "Nice meeting you, Maxine. Be a good friend for my Toni."

"Like Judson and Earle, or Bell and Ellis," Maxine said. "That's how it'll be."

"Good," Mrs. Skye said, slowly sitting back down. "Because Toni knows how tired I am."

"Grandma."

"And I don't always have the strength to take care of a young girl who keeps getting herself into too much trouble. Someday I might not—"

"I'll be right back, Grandma," Toni said, pulling Maxine toward the door.

"Nice meeting you, Mrs. Skye," Maxine said.

"Keep an eye on my granddaughter, Maxine," Mrs. Skye warned.

Reaching the street, Toni glanced down at the three dollars her grandmother had given her. She laughed softly to herself. Clutching the money in her fist, she began walking quickly back to school.

Reaching Thirty-ninth Avenue, with their school just down the block, Toni laughed again. "I think you're going to have to write to your friend Phil," she said.

"Why?" Maxine asked, trying to keep up with Toni's long strides.

"Because there's no way we're going to have any

inventing contest. I asked Mr. Seligman at morning lineup. He said it would take too much time, and we need to work on our basics."

"What's a basic?" Maxine asked.

"Math. Spelling. Map skills. The stuff everybody's supposed to know."

"Why does he need to teach us stuff everybody already knows?"

"That's what he said," Toni answered.

"But we have to start working on our invention soon," Maxine complained. "The deadline for entering the contest is October fifteenth."

"I think you're going to have to write that Phil friend of yours and tell him to talk to Mr. Seligman." Toni stopped walking and shoved the money into her pocket, then looked down at Maxine and smiled. "Because if my grandmother finds out we were lying, she's going to give me up."

"Maxine!" Wat shouted, running toward her. "They were going to put me in jail!"

"What happened?" Maxine asked, kneeling.

"You're late," he said angrily. "Mr. Swaboda, my after-school teacher, said, 'Children who get left get taken to the police station.' "

"I'm sorry," Maxine said, brushing Wat's hair out of his eyes.

"He was already mad at me," Wat continued, " 'cause I wasn't paying attention during storytime. But he wasn't even making up a story! He was just reading it from a book!"

"Maxine," Toni said, turning to leave. "Thanks."

"No problem." Maxine shrugged. She stood and took Wat's hand.

"C'mon," she said. "Let's go home. I'll tell you a story."

Maxine Candle
34-37 59th Drive
Woodside, Queens
New York, NY 11377

September 23

Phil Donahue
NBC
30 Rockefeller Center
New York, NY 10112

Dear Phil,

Well, it's been almost two weeks since my last letter, when I wrote to you right before I thought I was about to be beaten up by my new best friend for life, Toni. Two weeks, and you still haven't written to me. I can see you were really worried.

Then again, maybe you thought I was clever enough to figure out a way to avoid such an unpleasant event. If that's what you were thinking, you were right, sort of.

Instead of beating me up, Toni asked me

to come over to her house and meet her grandmother. Phil, Toni does not live in a nice neighborhood. I think somebody should invent a better place for a kid to live. Anyway, I met Toni's grandmother. She is not a happy person. I think this made me uncomfortable. I think it made me lose control of my imagination. I think I tried to make Toni's grandmother happy by making up a new Toni.

I told Mrs. Skye, Toni's grandmother, that Toni and I were best friends, that we were partners in the Inventions of Children Contest, and that we were going to win the contest and be on your show.

Now Toni's grandmother is waiting for all of this to happen. This is not good because Mr. Seligman, our teacher, has decided he doesn't want the class to do the Inventions of Children Contest. It interferes with us learning our basics.

I told Toni I would talk with you. I called your office. I spoke with Mrs. Johnson. She listened to me. She said you were busy. I told her it was important. We accidentally got disconnected. I called back. I accidentally got disconnected again. I called back. The same thing happened. I called three more times. Phil, either your secretary doesn't know how to use a hold button, or something is wrong with your phones.

I told Toni I spoke with you and that you had agreed to talk with Mr. Seligman and straighten everything out. I said this because Toni was looking sadder and sadder. I told her you were glad to hear from me. I don't think she believed me, but she sort of smiled. That was a week ago.

Yesterday, while we were going downstairs, Toni pushed me. When I turned around and asked her why she had done that, she told me she wanted me to hurry home to call my buddy Phil.

I told her I had just spoken to you on the phone again, and you had apologized for taking so much time.

When I turned around, she pushed me again.

So I threatened her. I told her I was going to cut her out of the chapter in my biography on my early years.

Phil, if you don't write to or talk to Mr. Seligman soon, it's not going to be safe for me to walk down the stairs. I'm also never going to become a famous inventor.

And I don't know what, but I think something bad is going to happen to Toni.

Just call Mr. Seligman at school. He teaches

at P.S. 205. His number is (718) 555-1313. Call him between twelve and one. Don't worry about ruining his lunch.

Sincerely,

*Maxine Candle*

Maxine Candle
34-37 59th Drive
Woodside, Queens
New York, NY 11377

September 25

Phil Donahue
NBC
30 Rockefeller Center
New York, NY 10112

Dear Phil,

You want to hurry up, already?

Toni is looking less and less happy these days. It's like she's trying to disappear, or at least trying to make everybody around her disappear. She moved her desk farther away from me, toward the back of the room. She ignores what Mr. Seligman assigns us. Mostly, she draws. She draws beds. Made-up beds, with the covers pulled high and folded over just beneath the pillows. Usually, her beds are empty, but sometimes she draws somebody in the bed with the covers pulled up to that person's eyes.

When she's not drawing, she does math. She works out of this thick, beat-up textbook. When Mr. Seligman calls on her, she just stares back at him and doesn't say anything. When I talk to her, she smiles, then looks away.

I keep thinking about something that Toni said. She said her grandmother was going to give her up.

This morning, when she went to the bathroom, I slid my desk back. I wanted to get closer to her. I also wanted to see what she was doing in that math book. When Mr. Seligman wasn't looking, I opened it. I tried to do some of the problems, but all of the equations had strange symbols, numbers with decimals, and too many letters, too many $x$'s and $n$'s. They looked like math problems Wat would invent.

In the yard during recess, I tried to talk to Toni, but she told me to go away. I left her sitting on her bench, facing the back of the yard. When I was walking away, another kid in my class, Shawnna, came up to me and asked me why I was always hanging out with Toni.

I told her Toni was my best friend.

Shawnna made a face like she was looking at a car accident. She told me I should have seen what Toni did to her best friend last year.

I walked away. I'm sure Toni's best friend last year wasn't an inventor.

That afternoon, when we were doing social studies, Mr. Seligman walked over to Toni's desk and picked up her math book. It was ninth-grade sequential math. Mr. Seligman smiled and said he didn't know we had a math scholar in the class.

Toni grabbed back her book and told him there was a lot he didn't know and was never going to know. Then she turned her chair completely around.

Phil, I think you're making her very cranky. I think she's giving up hope. How about a phone call? Just one phone call to Mr. Seligman. Have your secretary dial. You just talk. Talk, Phil, just talk.

Remember, the deadline for the contest is October fifteenth.

Sincerely,

Maxine Candle

Maxine Candle
34-37 59th Drive
Woodside, Queens
New York, NY 11377

September 29

Phil Donahue
NBC
30 Rockefeller Center
New York, NY 10112

Dear Phil,

Don't think just because you're ignoring me, and Toni's ignoring me, and Mr. Seligman is ignoring me, that I'm not doing anything. Today I invented a refrigerator that tells you what's inside it.

At least I almost invented it.

I almost invented it because Wat likes to open the refrigerator and stare inside it while he tries to figure out what he's going to eat. Wat can do this for a long time. He can stand there, his hand holding open the door, his face white in the refrigerator light and frost, for minutes, hours, even days. Usually when my mother sees him doing this, she says, "Wat, it's not a major motion picture. Open the door. Pick what you want. Close the door."

Sometimes I wonder if it's bad for his heart. I wonder if he stands there too long, can his heart freeze just like a snowball?

So, Phil, I did it. It took me two days, but I did it. I almost invented a talking refrigerator, which is just one more reason why you should call Mr. Seligman.

This is how it almost worked.

As soon as my mother went out, I took our phone message machine and erased my parents' message, which used to say, "You have reached the Candle home. Please leave a message."

In its place, I had Wat record a list of all the foods we had in our refrigerator. Wat's new message said, "Two slices of ham. Three eggs. A little milk. Almost no orange juice. Something in tinfoil. Something that looks like soup. Three oranges. Something that looks like a lot of vegetables all mixed together."

Then I put the message machine into the refrigerator.

All Wat had to do was call our number, and the machine turned on, and his own voice told him what was inside. No more getting yelled at. No more chance of getting his heart frozen.

It almost worked.

Maybe, Phil, you could have me on your

show and I could discuss how it almost worked.

I was also wondering, Phil—have you lost my number? Are you getting any of these letters? Why aren't you writing back?

Well? Time is running out. Help!

Sincerely yours,

*Maxine Candle*

# ☆ 7 ☆

# A Letter from Home

## *October 1*

Sitting at the kitchen table, helping Wat do his homework and waiting for her mother, Maxine realized she needed a letter from home. A letter from her mother urging Mr. Seligman to have the contest. Her mother could write about all of Maxine's great inventions. Her mother could convince Mr. Seligman Maxine was for real.

"We're learning about families," Wat explained, leaning over the kitchen table. He turned his notebook upside down and slid it across the table to Maxine. She skimmed through the pages. They were filled with Wat's drawings and cut-out pages from magazines. Each picture had two labels, one written by Mrs. Finch in correct English, the other written by her brother in Wat English. Under a picture of a lion, Mrs. Finch had written, in blue crayon, "Cats eat meat." Wat had written, "Kitz et met."

"Today we learned about grandmothers," Wat explained. "I said I have one grandma who lives in Florida and one who lives in Shea Stadium."

"Near Shea Stadium." Maxine laughed. "She's not a shortstop. She lives near the stadium."

"That's what Mrs. Finch said—'Near. Near.' But Daniel brought his in for show-and-tell."

"That's nice," she said, not listening. She wondered when her mother would arrive. Would she write the letter? What if she refused?

"He did," Wat insisted.

"Did what?" Maxine asked.

"Bring his grandma in. For show-and-tell. And she did a dance. And Nadine brought in a fish."

"Nadine's grandmother is a fish?"

"No!" Wat explained, surprised by Maxine's foolishness. "Her grandmother caught a fish. It was a sunfish. It was flat and shiny, and it had red and blue on it, and it was about this big." Wat held his hands a few inches apart. "And after, Nadine poured water in its mouth, and when she squeezed its belly, it spit!"

"Sounds entertaining." Maxine smiled.

"You have to write down there"—Wat pointed to the book. "I have to tell you a story about us, and you have to write it down. Then I have to copy it."

"What story do you want to tell me?" Maxine asked.

"I want to tell the story about the time Daddy took Mommy and me and you to Alley Pond Park to teach us the trees, and it rained."

"I'm home!" their mother called, stepping into the apartment. "Did anybody call?"

Grabbing Wat's notebook and a crayon, Maxine followed him into the living room.

"Hello, Wat! Hello, Maxie!" their mother said, leaning over and hugging them with her free arm. Her other arm was loaded with thick reports from her students. "Did anybody call? I'm expecting an important call."

Suddenly Maxine felt as if she had swallowed an ice cube. "Call?" she asked. "You mean on the phone?"

"Yes, on the phone," her mother said, looking curiously at Maxine. "Or on the machine. Did anyone leave any messages?"

Her mother would never write the letter. Wat looked down at the carpet.

"The first problem," Maxine explained, handing Wat back his book and following her mother toward the dining room, "was that we had to wait for somebody to call to hear what was inside."

"Inside what?" her mother asked.

"She wouldn't let me open the door and peek," Wat added, following Maxine. "I only wanted to look."

"Look at what?" her mother asked.

"I tried a new experiment," Maxine said softly. "For Wat. I put the phone and the phone machine in the refrigerator."

"But did anybody call?" her mother asked, apparently not hearing her. Reaching the dining room, she cleared a space on her desk and dropped her reports with a loud *thump*. The small dining area, attached to their living room, had been turned into an office. In addition to her mother's rolltop desk, there were filing cabinets and a small couch. It was Maxine's favorite place. When she wanted to feel intelligent and her mother was not home, Maxine would sit at the desk, then suddenly spin around on the swivel chair, hold up her finger, and shout, "Aha! Aha! That's it!"

"Who tried to reach us?" her mother asked.

"Who?" Maxine answered, sitting on the small couch and pulling her knees up to her chest. "Who tried to reach us? Oh . . . you want to hear the second problem? The second problem was when somebody called, we had to open the refrigerator door, pick up the phone, and try to convince who called that they had reached the right number."

Her mother picked up a stack of papers from the floor beneath the desk. Sitting on the swivel chair, she placed her reports in a tall pile and spun around to face Maxine and Wat.

"Maxine," she asked patiently, "did anybody call?"

"Yes. Uncle Jeff," Maxine remembered. "He said he once had something in his refrigerator that looked like a lot of vegetables all mixed together. He said when he tried to eat it, it ran off his table and out of his apartment onto Pelham Parkway."

Her mother looked puzzled. "Did anyone else call?"

"Dad called," Wat said, sitting on the floor and opening his book.

"Your father called? What did he say?"

"He said," Wat remembered, " 'Don't eat the thing that looks like soup. It used to be a chicken potpie.' "

"He also said he'd be home about two or three tonight," Maxine added, "from that wedding up at Ramapo."

Her mother removed a ruler from her top desk drawer and held it against her reports. She measured the height of the stack. "Did anyone else call besides your father?"

"You're not upset about the phone?" Maxine asked cautiously.

"Eighteen inches," her mother said to herself, measuring the stack. "Eighteen inches of reports on modern American poets. That's about one inch a poet, one half hour an inch. I'm going to be up marking these papers until your father gets home."

"So you're not upset about my message?" Maxine asked again.

"Maxine." Her mother leaned forward in her chair. She held Maxine's hands. "I imagine I could tell you not to experiment with our phone machine or anything that belongs to the grown-ups in the house. How does that sound?"

"Ma, I need you to write a letter."

"You didn't answer my question," her mother said. "How does not experimenting with anything that belongs to the grown-ups sound?"

"That sounds reasonable," Maxine said.

"Does it sound like something you would do?"

"I did it for Wat," she said defensively. "I didn't want him to get too cold staring into the refrigerator. I thought the cold might be bad for his heart."

"Maxine." Her mother sighed. "All I want you to do for Wat is be a fun older sister. Tell him stories. Help him with his homework over milk and cookies."

"Mrs. Finch said we can't eat cookies for a snack," Wat explained, looking up from his notebook, "because there's sugar in them, and that's not healthy, and it can make you act wild and make your teeth fall out."

Maxine glanced over at Wat's paper. She tried to guess whether he had been drawing or writing. There were too many green and blue swervy lines that could be waves, birds, or even letters.

"Wat, I think Mrs. Finch got a little carried away," their mother said. "I don't think two cookies and milk are going to cause a five-year-old to become uncontrollable."

"She said, 'Cookies make you crazy.' She said that."

"What will she let you eat?"

"Something from the five major food groups. She showed us pictures," Wat said, trying to remember. "I think they were cow foods, chicken foods, Cheerios, crayons, and Christopher Columbus."

"Those were Mrs. Finch's five major food groups?" their mother asked, amused.

"Wat," Maxine said, also amused, "I think those were *c* words. I think you looked at the wrong board.

*Cookies, crazy*—those are *c* words. I don't think Mrs. Finch wants anyone to bring in crayons for a snack."

"Or Columbus," her mother added.

"Oh," Wat said, returning to his notebook.

"Who else called?" her mother asked.

"A lady called," Wat said, taking back his book.

"Do you remember her name?" their mother asked.

"No," Maxine apologized.

"Do you remember what she wanted?"

"She wanted to know what was inside the tinfoil," Wat said, switching to a red crayon.

Maxine stared at the curves, squiggles, and crazy assortment of vowels and consonants. "Why are you switching crayons?" she asked Wat.

"Red is for the scary words," he explained, not bothering to look up.

"Maxine, I think you should stay away from anything in the house you think is too valuable to tinker with."

"I don't tinker," Maxine insisted.

"Experiment," her mother corrected herself. "I didn't mean tinker. I meant experiment. When your father and I are not home, you should avoid experimenting with things like the phone machine, the stereo . . ."

"The stereo?" Maxine said, her feelings hurt. "All I wanted to do was make it possible for Wat to talk back to the man in the radio station. I figured if Wat could hear him, then he should be able to hear Wat. In case of an emergency, Wat could say something like 'I need help.' Then the man on the radio could tell all his listeners."

Her mother took a deep breath. "Maxine, why can't you just experiment as a hobby?"

"A hobby?" Maxine asked, aghast. "Knitting is a hobby! Raising tropical fish is a hobby! Nobody becomes famous from a hobby."

"Maxine," her mother said, leaning over and whispering to her so Wat couldn't hear, "your experimenting is drawing too much attention to Wat's heart, and I'd rather he not think of it at all. Stop inventing things for him. You're making him more worried. I know you mean well, but you're not helping. Why can't you just make inventing your hobby?"

"Nobody changes the world with a hobby," Maxine mumbled. "Nobody helps anybody."

Her mother leaned back in her chair. "Why don't you just be an older sister, Maxine? Help Wat with his homework."

"I'm going to," she said angrily. Sitting on the floor, she reached over and took Wat's notebook and crayon from him.

"You want me to write down that story?" she asked him. "About the time Daddy took us to the park and taught us the trees?"

Wat nodded. "Yes."

"Then Mommy will sign it?" Maxine asked, loud enough for her mother to hear.

"Why do I need to sign your homework, Wat?" their mother asked.

Wat looked up at Maxine, then to their mother, then back to Maxine.

Maxine turned to Wat so her mother couldn't see and mouthed, "Make it up."

"Because . . . we're studying families . . . and Mrs. Finch wants to make sure our families are paying attention."

Maxine smiled at her brother.

"Of course I'll sign it," their mother said, returning to her work.

"One day it was wet and slippery out, and my daddy took us to the park," Wat said, sitting up. "I wore a yellow raincoat with boots. Maxine wore her baseball cap. Mommy took the umbrella. We saw squirrels and birds, and Daddy showed us the sycamore tree has skin that comes off."

"Bark, it's that bark flakes off," Maxine corrected.

"Bark, and the birch tree has bark that's white and you can use it for paper, and the maple tree has seeds that you can stick on your nose. That's what I want you to write."

"No problem," Maxine said, taking the crayon and writing. She repeated what Wat had told her, then wrote,

> Dear Mr. Seligman,
>     This is just to inform you that it is very important for my daughter to compete in the Inventions of Children Contest. It is more important than her homework. It is more im-

portant than her classwork. She has invented
at home for many years. All of her inventions
have been wonderful and useful. Phil Donahue is waiting for her to be on his show to
display her inventions. She needs to become
a famous inventor, and learning the basics will
just make her like anybody else. Please let
her enter the contest. Her partner is Toni
Skye.

Sincerely yours,

Standing up, she tapped her mother on the shoulder
and presented her with the notebook. "He just needs
you to sign it here," Maxine said, offering her mother
Wat's notebook and the crayon.

"Sure," her mother said, and without looking, signed
the paper.

"Here, Wat," Maxine said, delighted. She turned the
page and gave Wat back his book. "Now, why don't
you tell me that story again, and I'll help you copy it
over."

"One day," Wat began, "it was wet and slippery . . ."

# Inventing Problems

## October 2

axine waited. Half listening to Mr. Seligman explain again the difference between the numerator and the denominator, she wondered what he would say after she showed him the letter. How could he argue with her mother?

She just wished she had it with her. After helping Wat write his real homework, his story about the time they visited the woods, she had forgotten to rip her mother's letter out of Wat's notebook. By the time she remembered, Wat had packed it away and fallen asleep. She couldn't get it in the morning, either. For some reason her mother had decided to walk them to school, making it impossible for Maxine to get the letter out of Wat's book bag.

First glancing down at his teacher's edition, Mr. Seligman looked back up at the board and drew two pizza pies on it. He explained they both had diameters of eight inches.

"These pies are the exact same size," he read out loud from his teacher's manual. Then he divided the first pie into four slices. He divided the second pie into eight slices. Maxine knew what he was going to ask next.

"Again," Mr. Seligman reminded them, "these pies are exactly the same size. But the first pie is divided into four slices, and the second pie is divided into eight slices. Which pie has more to eat?"

"The one with the extra cheese," somebody in the back called out.

A few kids laughed. Mr. Seligman grimaced. Victor was the only student to raise a hand. Mr. Seligman pretended not to see him. Maxine knew why. Victor was just going to repeat what he had said yesterday. And the day before. She also knew that nobody else in the class was going to raise a hand because they were all brain dead. Mr. Seligman had killed them with boredom. Basics!

"The pie with the four slices?" Mr. Seligman read out loud from his manual. "Or the pie with eight slices?" Again he searched the classroom for somebody other than Victor to raise a hand.

There wasn't anybody.

"Victor?"

"The pie with eight slices," Victor proudly declared.

Mr. Seligman looked defeated. He leaned back against the chalkboard. "Why is that, Victor?" he asked sadly.

"Because it's got more slices," Victor pointed out, as if Mr. Seligman were blind. "Eight's more than four."

Somebody in the back giggled. Mr. Seligman turned around and stared at his pies. He glanced back down at his manual and ran his finger across something that was written there. Maxine watched him move his lips as he read silently to himself. She leaned over to Toni and tapped her desk. Toni looked up from her notes and rolled her eyes.

"So," Maxine whispered, "you're still going to be my partner in the contest?"

Toni grinned. She leaned over to Maxine. "Listen," she whispered, "my grandmother wants to know how come I haven't brought you back again. She said you're a good influence on me." She checked Mr. Seligman to make sure he wasn't watching. "Maxine," she whispered, "I don't know what's going to happen, but that was a nice thing you did for me."

"It was almost the truth," Maxine insisted.

"Very *almost*." Toni laughed.

"It's just too bad Wat wasn't there," Maxine added.

"Why?"

"He could have taken pictures. We could have passed them around on Phil's show."

Toni's smile disappeared. "What's with you?" she asked, sliding her desk away from Maxine. "All you care about is your nonsense about being famous. What is it? You can't do something just because it's a nice thing to do?"

"But I was—" Maxine started to protest.

"Well," Mr. Seligman announced, loudly clearing his throat, "if that's all understood, then I guess you should open your books to page 95 and do the whole page."

Maxine put her hands in her desk and tugged on her math book. It was stuck. She yanked it out, along with some crumpled papers that fell to the floor around her. Hurriedly she bent to pick them up and bumped her head on the bottom of her desk. Wincing from the pain, her eyes tearing, she gathered the papers together and sat up, careful to avoid smashing her head again. She opened her book and tried to find the right page. Her fingers felt stupid and clumsy. Page 93 was stuck to page 95. She tried to separate them and ripped page 93 in half. She shoved the torn piece into her desk and examined the work. Equations. No words. Not thinking. Simple additions and subtractions of fractions. Thousands of them. Millions of them. They went on forever. She would spend the rest of her life adding and subtracting fractions. She would turn old. She would lose her teeth. She would die doing them. She spent a minute or two on the first few problems. Reaching the fifth problem, she closed her eyes and tried to solve the problem without looking.

"You too, Toni," Mr. Seligman said sternly.

Maxine opened her right eye, just enough to see Mr. Seligman standing over Toni and pointing his finger at her loose-leaf notebook.

"I want something to show your grandmother when

she comes for parent-teacher"—he corrected himself—
"for teacher conferences."

Sullenly, Toni removed the class's math book from
inside her desk and opened it to page 95. Cursing Mr.
Seligman under her breath, she popped open her loose-
leaf notebook and glanced at the problems.

After pausing a few seconds, she wrote down the
answer to the first problem.

Maxine checked her own work to see if Toni's answer was correct. It was. In another few seconds, Toni
answered the second, third, fourth, and fifth problems.
She just wrote down the answers. She didn't bother
to copy the problems. No scratch work. She looked at
the problem. She answered it. Just like that. To Maxine's amazement, Toni answered the next ten problems just as quickly and as effortlessly as the first.

Making sure Mr. Seligman wasn't watching her,
Maxine removed her calculator and checked Toni's answers as she did them. They were all correct. She
watched Toni attack a long word problem, the only one
on the page. Maxine raced Toni to the answer, using
her calculator. Toni was quicker. But just as accurate.
It was as if Toni knew the right way to look at a
problem so that the answer would pop up and reveal
itself.

"So . . . you'll be my partner in the contest?"

Toni put down her pencil and looked at Maxine as if
there were a strange language written across her face.
"I told you. There isn't going to be an Inventions of
Children Contest."

Maxine smiled confidently. "But if there is—" She winked. "I think I can make it happen."

"You would," Toni dismissed her. "You think you can do anything."

"But that's the way inventors are supposed to think," Maxine said. "I read in one of my inventing and discovering books that when James Watson was a kid, he wanted to solve a problem that would win him the Nobel Prize. So he went and discovered DNA."

"Who's James Watson?" Toni asked.

"I don't know," Maxine admitted. "I don't even know what DNA is. But I like to think the way James Watson thought."

Toni wasn't listening. She turned her desk away from Maxine, back toward the window.

Maxine looked up at the clock. It was eleven-thirty. In forty-five minutes, she would pick up Wat with his writing notebook. Together they would find Mr. Seligman. He would probably be in the teachers' cafeteria. She would ask him to come out for a minute. She would show him the letter from her mother. He would agree to let her enter the contest.

She pushed aside her math book. Forty-five minutes. She could use that time for more important things. She could practice signing her autograph.

She opened to a clean page in her writing section, removed her pen from its case, and began to experiment with the slant of her script and the curve of her *M* and *C*. She had a problem. She couldn't decide whether to settle on a clear, precise signature or a sloppy one. She thought of the people who would one day want her autograph. A clear signature would be good for her fans, who would want to be able to read her name and show it to others to prove they had met her. A sloppy autograph, though, would give people the impression she was too busy and important inventing things and thinking about inventing things to sign autographs. She liked that. For the next fifteen minutes she practiced making her handwriting illegible. Then she stopped. She liked her name. It was a good name. Written neatly, it already looked famous without her.

She glanced up at the clock again. It was eleven forty-five. She was getting impatient. She noticed Elisa in front of her, passing a note to Shawna. Maxine could read something about a game during lunch. She wondered why Elisa wasn't using the invisible ink Maxine had invented and offered to her. Made out of milk and lemon juice, it became invisible after you finished writing your message. Then it stayed invisible forever.

Demonstrating her invention during the first week of school, Maxine had written, "Elisa, I'll meet you in the yard during recess." She had never invented anything before for anybody but Wat. Maybe inventing for other kids would be a good way to make friends. "See," she said, showing Elisa the blank piece of paper. They were in the back of the auditorium.

They were supposed to be watching a film on self-esteem. "Invisible ink. It works. You can write notes with it."

"But I can't read what you wrote," Elisa had answered.

"That's because it's invisible," Maxine said proudly.

"But then nobody's going to be able to read what I write," Elisa pointed out.

"So?" Maxine didn't understand why that was a problem. "Just whisper to them what you wrote."

"If I'm going to whisper anyway, then why should I write a note in the first place? Why would I need invisible ink?"

"Because I invented it."

"You are too weird," Elisa said, and turned her back to Maxine.

Now Maxine tried to read more of the note over Elisa's shoulder. There was a list of girls' names on it. Hers wasn't. That didn't surprise her. The other girls thought her talk about inventions was boring and silly. They didn't believe her when she talked about Phil. They moved away from her when she sat next to them during lunch.

"Your brother still having trouble napping?"

Maxine looked up. It was Toni. She was holding her math textbook and answer sheet in her hands, ready to take them to Mr. Seligman.

"Yup," Maxine said. "He won't sleep in class."

"Well"—Toni laughed, pointing to her work—"this

would have put him to sleep." She took a step toward the front of the class.

"Wait." Maxine grabbed Toni's hand. "If . . . if I get him"—she pointed to Mr. Seligman—"if I get him to let us have the contest, will you be my partner? Will you come over this afternoon so we can start talking about our ideas?"

Toni looked toward Mr. Seligman's desk. He was quietly talking to himself, marking papers. She turned back to Maxine.

"Why do you keep at it?" Toni asked her. "Why did you pick me? Why do you want to be my friend?"

"Because . . . because that's the way it's supposed to be."

"I have to bring these papers up to Mr. Seligman."

Maxine watched Toni approach Mr. Seligman's desk. Mr. Seligman didn't seem happy to see her.

"What can I do for you?" he asked. The class was so quiet, Maxine could hear him all the way in the back.

"I'm done," Toni said, laying her paper on his desk.

"Good," Mr. Seligman said, putting a mark in his teacher's book. Quickly he marked Toni's paper, checking her answers against the answers in his manual. It looked to Maxine as if Toni had gotten them all correct. "Good," Mr. Seligman repeated, looking up at the clock. He turned back to Toni. "Well done. Now do the next page."

Maxine watched Toni open her math book and glance at the next page. "That's another twenty-five problems," Toni said, not moving. She closed the book and rested it on top of a pile of papers on Mr. Seligman's desk. Taking a deep breath, she put her hands on her hips and stared out the windows for a moment. She turned back to Mr. Seligman. "You're kidding, right?" she asked.

"No," Mr. Seligman said flatly. "You finished the first page. Now do the next."

Toni picked up her book. She began to tap her foot. With her skinny arms bent, with her long fingers on her hips and her long, skinny legs slightly bowed, she reminded Maxine of a spider, an angry spider.

"You know I got the first twenty-five problems all right."

"Good," Mr. Seligman said again.

"I understood them the first time," Toni said, her voice beginning to sound angry. "I didn't need to listen to you explain how to do them, and I still got them all right. You think doing the same thing twenty-five more times is going to make me any smarter?"

"Return to your seat, Toni," Mr. Seligman said, not showing any emotion. "Do as I say."

"No."

"Do what I tell you, or I will have to call your grandmother tonight."

"We don't have a phone." Toni grabbed her book. "But you could try calling," she said, striding back to her desk. "Try it about twenty-five times. Maybe by the twenty-fifth time, you'll get through." She sat.

"You just got yourself a note home," Mr. Seligman said. "And I don't think your grandmother is going to be too pleased with what I'm going to write."

Toni leaned back in her chair and smiled defiantly at Mr. Seligman. She turned to Maxine. "So how about this afternoon?" she asked. "You want me to come over this afternoon?"

"Sure," Maxine said, not really meaning it. "We can start . . ." Maxine paused. Toni looked as if she was about to cry. "We can start to plan our invention."

## ☆ 9 ☆

# The Law

## *Later That Same Day*

**66I**s it the law?" Wat asked, following Maxine out of the cafeteria.

"You have your notebook?" Maxine asked. "The one with your homework about our family?"

"Is it the law?" Wat repeated.

"Is what the law?"

"Napping. Is nap time the law? We had a substitute today, Mrs. Fowler, and I didn't want to nap, and Berto didn't want to nap, and Tamara and Runis didn't want to nap because I didn't want to nap, and Mrs. Fowler got angry, and she said I had to nap. Then Justin said he didn't want to nap. And Mrs. Fowler got more angry, and said I had to nap. She said, 'Nap time is the law.' She said that."

"So you didn't nap?" Maxine asked, holding the third-floor door open for her brother.

"I don't want to nap," Wat said, walking under his sister's arm. His hands were full with his dinosaur lunch box and his writing pad. "I don't want to close my eyes," he said, trying to keep up with Maxine as she swiftly walked through the corridor. "I get bad dreams when I sleep in the daytime."

"You get bad dreams at night, too," Maxine said.

"But I get worse dreams in the daytime. I don't like lying down and going to sleep when everybody is around me. Somebody could do something. It's scary. Is it against the law?"

They reached the door to the teachers' cafeteria. Yellow paper curtains hung from the windows of the door, making it difficult to see who was inside. Rising on her toes, Maxine could barely make out the face of Mrs. Krill. She was the reading teacher for the kids who had trouble reading. Mrs. Krill had an overstuffed, round face and thick glasses kids said she used like magnifying lenses to burn tiny holes on the back of your hands if you were bad. She was holding a forkful of cottage cheese in front of her lips. It looked as if she was explaining something. Maxine tried to see if Mr. Seligman was in there.

"Is it against the law?" Wat asked. "Because what happens if you're napping, and the teacher goes to sleep, and somebody strange comes into the room?" Wat tugged on Maxine's sleeve. "What if?"

"Wat, nobody is going to sneak into your room when you're napping."

"You don't know that," Wat insisted.

"We have a school security guard."

"But the person could look nice. He could look like a doctor. What if he just came in when everybody was sleeping, and he saw me? What if he watched me when I was napping?"

"Wat, your imagination is too wild. Nobody is going to do that."

"And what if I get bad dreams? What if I'm in class, and I get bad dreams?"

"Wat," Maxine said, kneeling beside him next to the door to the teachers' cafeteria, "what kind of bad dreams do you get?"

"Sometimes," Wat said, looking up at a bulletin board display showing in paper cutouts the *Niña*, the *Pinta*, and the *Santa Maria*, "I get dreams that black birds are sitting on my chest and they won't go away. And sometimes, I get dreams that I can't find you."

"Me?" Maxine asked. "You can't find me?"

Wat nodded.

"But we're always together. Even when you're in class, I'm just two floors away. I'm always near."

"Not when I close my eyes," Wat said. "I don't like closing my eyes in the daytime. It makes everybody far away."

"I'm always right here," Maxine said, giving Wat a hug, then standing. She held her finger to her lips, slowly turned the handle, and pushed open the door just enough to hear a man say, "But she's such a smart kid. There's something very special about her. I wish she liked me." It was Mr. Seligman's voice.

"Who said she's supposed to like you?" Mrs. Krill asked. "You're supposed to be her teacher, not her friend, especially with a kid like Toni Skye."

"I still think it would work. She's great at math. If she tutors Victor, she might help Victor, and it'll make her feel better about herself. I think that's the problem."

"Listen, you're her teacher, not her social worker."

"But she's so angry. If I write that letter, she'll just get angrier. It won't work. I want her to enjoy coming to class."

"Who said she's supposed to enjoy it?" Mrs. Krill asked. "You're a teacher, not an entertainer."

"But I'm not enjoying teaching."

"I haven't enjoyed teaching in twenty years," Mrs. Krill admitted, gulping down a mouthful of cottage cheese. "It's a job. You get your summers off. You go home at three."

"I didn't want it to be just a job. I wanted to teach. I wanted to reach kids like Victor and Toni. Sometimes I wonder if any of them are learning anything."

"We're not," Maxine whispered to Wat.

"Maxine, I don't want to do it," he said.

"Listen," Maxine whispered. "I'm going to invent something for you. And this time it's going to work. Mom and Dad are going to be proud. Just do what I asked. Please?"

Taking a deep breath, Wat pushed open the door and walked over to Mr. Seligman.

Mrs. Krill immediately stood, her mouth overflowing with cottage cheese. "And what are you doing in here?" she angrily demanded. "That sign says 'teachers' cafeteria.' Can't you read?"

Wat thought about it. "I can almost read," he said. "In Mrs. Finch's class I almost read 'The cat eats meat,' and I can read my name. And I think I can read the word *chicken*. It starts with a *c*, right?"

"No children are allowed in here." Mrs. Krill pointed to the door.

Wat looked back over his shoulder. He couldn't see Maxine. She was hiding.

"I said no children are allowed in here," Mrs. Krill reminded him.

"If you yell at me again," Wat said, looking up at her, "I'm going to tell my teacher you didn't nap today."

Mrs. Krill snorted.

Wat turned to Mr. Seligman. "You have to come with me into the hall. It's important."

"What happened?" Mr. Seligman asked, looking concerned.

"My sister . . ." Wat started to say.

"Who is your sister?" Mr. Seligman asked, wiping some tuna salad from the corners of his mouth.

"She's almost . . . Stay here!" Wat shouted at Mr. Seligman, then ran back out into the hallway.

Maxine was crouched against the wall by the door.

"Well?" she asked Wat.

"He's not coming," Wat told her.

"Mention Phil, tell him about Phil," Maxine urged, pushing Wat back into the cafeteria.

"Phil Donahue's almost in the hallway," Wat said.

Mr. Seligman stood, dropping a dab of tuna salad onto his shirt. "Oh no," he moaned, wiping, then spreading the stain with his napkin. "I think I know who your sister is.

"Hello, Maxine," Mr. Seligman called out into the hallway, looking and sounding cheerless. He nervously dabbed at the stain on his shirt with his crumpled napkin. "Where is she?"

"You know," Maxine said, pushing herself up along the wall, "I once almost invented something that could get that out."

"What can I do for you, Maxine?" Mr. Seligman asked. "This is my lunch hour."

"Here," Maxine said. "Now you have to let us have the contest. Wat, show it to him. Show him the letter."

Putting his dinosaur pack down at his feet, Wat opened his notebook, skimmed through the pages, found what he was looking for, and showed it to Mr. Seligman.

Reluctantly Mr. Seligman took Wat's book and began to read.

"See, it's all there. Everything about Phil. Everything about me being an inventor. Everything about how important it is to have the contest," Maxine argued. "And my mother signed it."

To Maxine's surprise, Mr. Seligman began to smile. He seemed fascinated by what he was reading.

"Mr. Seligman," Maxine said joyfully, "I promise. It's all true!"

"I can tell that. I can," Mr. Seligman agreed, grinning broadly. He turned the page, turned it back, then closed the book and patted Wat's head.

"You're some writer, Wat," Mr. Seligman said.

"Thank you," Wat said. "I could only write three letters, but my mother said that was all right. She said I didn't have to be in a hurry to learn how to write."

"I don't understand," Maxine said, growing anxious. "What are you talking about, Wat?"

"I copied over what you wrote, Maxie," Wat said proudly. "Mommy liked it. She read what you wrote, then she told me to copy it over."

Maxine lunged for the book. Mr. Seligman pulled it away.

"So, Maxine," Mr. Seligman said, turning his back to Maxine and opening the book again and glancing down at Wat's writing, "you think if I allow the class to compete in the Inventions of Children Contest, the kids will start enjoying themselves a little more?"

"Yes, especially me and Toni. She's my partner," Maxine said, feeling her face get hotter and hotter. What had her brother written? What was Mr. Seligman reading? What did her mother see?

"You and Toni?" Mr. Seligman looked back into the cafeteria at Mrs. Krill, then whispered confidentially to Maxine, "You think if I said yes, you could encourage your friend Toni to do a little math tutoring?"

Maxine nodded.

"Hmmm." Mr. Seligman smiled. "You really think the kids will like me more?"

"Yes," Maxine said, glancing at Wat. He was beaming with pride.

"See, I can write," he told Maxine.

"Maybe," Mr. Seligman wondered out loud, "maybe by working on your own inventions and confronting your problems, you will all actually learn something. You think that's true, Maxine?"

"Yes," Maxine mumbled.

"You don't sound enthusiastic anymore, Maxine," Mr. Seligman teased her. "What about your friend Phil? When you're on his show, you think you'll remember to mention me?"

"When I'm on Phil's show," Maxine said, suddenly wondering if Mr. Seligman was sincere, "I'll mention your name twice. And . . . and I'll tell his studio audience, and his viewers at home, that . . . that the whole class *liked* you."

"You'll say that?" Mr. Seligman asked.

Maxine nodded.

"And you'll mention my name?"

"Twice," Maxine said, trying to read Mr. Seligman's eyes. Was he pulling her leg?

"I'd like that." Mr. Seligman smiled. "Maxine, can I ask you one question?"

"Go ahead."

"Did you read this page of your . . . *evidence*?" Mr.

Seligman handed Maxine Wat's notebook, opened to the page he had read. "Did you look at it before you showed it to me?"

Maxine glared at Wat. "I didn't get a chance."

"Oh." Mr. Seligman laughed, stepping back into the cafeteria. "Well, you should read it. Your brother is some inventor himself."

Maxine stared down at the open page.

"See you after lunch," Mr. Seligman said, and gently closed the door behind him.

She could feel Wat leaning against her, standing on his toes to see what he had written.

"I wrote what you said?" he asked, peering over her arm at a page of blue scrawls, squiggles, and dots. "I can write?"

Maxine studied the page closely. She could make out a big *W*. Maybe that curved line was an *a*. She turned the page. More scribbles, this time in green. She turned back to the first page. Examining it more closely, she found a *t*. She looked for the letter she had written. She found where it had been torn out from the book.

"Wat, Mom saw what I wrote in your book?"

Wat nodded.

"Was she angry?" Maxine asked.

"She told me not to tell you," Wat said.

Wat lowered himself from his tiptoes and looked up at Maxine. He seemed to consider some idea, then said, "She also told me not to tell you she's taking me after lunch to Dr. Stone for my checkup."

"Without me?" Maxine asked. "Why?"

"She said you worry too much, and she didn't want you to miss school."

"But you're going to be scared without me. You need me," she argued.

"Mommy said not to tell you," Wat said, taking Maxine's hand. "Don't tell her I told you. She said she would bring me back by three so you could take me home."

"Wat, don't be scared," Maxine said, trying to sound calm and reassuring. "Everything will be fine. I don't want you to be scared."

"Maxine, I can write?"

"Almost," Maxine said, squeezing his hand. "Almost."

# ☆ 10 ☆

# Questions and Answers

## *That Afternoon*

Her mother and father were seated at the kitchen table when she brought Toni home.

"Oh, hello, Maxine," her father said, sounding tired. After glancing one more time at the front and back of some form, he pushed himself up from his chair.

"Where's Wat?" Maxine asked, suddenly noticing all the papers scattered over the kitchen table. "I went to pick him up at three, and his substitute teacher said you never brought him back."

"We were too busy trying to sell him to a traveling circus." Her father sighed.

"Or any passing strangers," her mother added. "My silly knight stories didn't work. He didn't behave himself too well at the doctor's today. We had quite an adventure trying to get him to lie still for the test."

"The echocardiogram looked more like an earthquake reading," her father said, walking over to Maxine and giving her a kiss on the top of her head. He

116

smiled pleasantly at Toni and offered her his hand. "And you are?"

"Toni, Toni Skye," she said, and politely shook his hand.

"What happened at the doctor's?" Maxine asked, looking first to her father, then her mother. "Where's Wat?"

Her mother turned around in her chair. Her eyes were red. She smiled at Toni. "Hello, Toni," she said. "Would you like to join us for dinner?"

"Thanks," Toni said. "But I can't. I have to get back to my grandmother." Toni shrugged.

"What happened at the doctor's?" Maxine asked again.

"Nothing," her father said, waving away the possibility of any problems. "Nothing. Wat wasn't too happy. We put him on the table and he flopped about like a fish out of water."

"What about his heart?" Maxine asked, staring at her mother.

"I would guess it's fine. We're just going to have to take him back for another test. This one was completely useless." Her mother sighed. She picked up some papers from the table. "We're just figuring out some forms. Why don't you and Toni take something to eat, then go help your brother with his homework?"

"Toni's my inventing partner," Maxine announced. She waited for her parents to jump up and cheer. "For the contest."

"That's nice," her mother said, writing something down on a form.

"That sounds exciting," her father said, flipping through the pages in a thick green booklet. He leaned over to her mother and asked her softly, "Do you think the insurance will cover . . ."

"We're entering the contest," Maxine declared, speaking louder than before.

"Good, good, I'm glad to hear that," her father said with false cheer. "I'm sure you'll win." Again he whispered something to her mother.

"Maxine," Toni urged, pulling on Maxine's sleeve. "Let's go find your brother and get our homework done. Before I have to leave."

Wat was lying on his belly on the floor on Maxine's side of their room. He was coloring in a page from a workbook. He had his crayons lined up in a neat row beside him.

"What happened at Dr. Stone's?" Maxine asked.

Wat sat up and looked suspiciously at Toni.

"Remember me?" Toni laughed. "You took my picture in the schoolyard."

Wat nodded.

"I'm sorry if I scared you. I was in a bad mood."

Wat looked at Maxine for clues.

"How are you doing?" Toni asked, sitting on the floor beside him.

Wat inched away from her.

"Wat, what happened at Dr. Stone's?" Maxine asked, sitting on the floor beside Toni.

Wat looked suspiciously at Toni. "I got scared again."

"Did anything go wrong?" Maxine asked.

"I don't know."

"Nothing went wrong?" Maxine asked.

"I don't know!" Wat said, growing angry. "Could you help me with my homework, Maxine?" He placed his workbook on her lap. "I need help."

"Why did you get scared?" Maxine asked again.

"Maxine," Wat insisted, "I need to do my homework. Mrs. Fowler said, 'Homework is the law, too.' If I don't do it, she's really going to put me in jail."

"Now, that's a strict kindergarten teacher." Toni laughed.

Maxine looked down at Wat's workbook. Scattered over the page were different-size sets of fruit, shoes, cars, airplanes, and other objects. Also scattered about were the words for different numbers.

Maxine guessed Wat was supposed to connect the numbers to the appropriate set of objects. "You're supposed to draw a line"—she showed Wat— "from the number to the picture that shows that many."

"Oh," Wat said, clearly lost.

"Like the number three," Toni said, leaning over the workbook. "Which picture shows the number three?"

Still wary of Toni, Wat pointed to the picture of the three clowns.

"Correct!" Toni said, patting him on the back. "Good work!"

Wat looked up to Maxine for her approval. "That's it," she repeated. "That's what you do."

"Oh," Wat said, and taking the book off Maxine's lap, lay down on his belly and grabbed a red crayon.

Clearing their own spaces, Maxine and Toni also lay down and began their homework.

"A car leaves Texas and drives to Chicago," Maxine started to read. "If it travels at sixty . . ." She turned to watch Toni. Toni was already writing down the answer. Maxine turned back to Wat.

"I don't understand," she told him. "What are you afraid of?"

"I don't know," Wat said, drawing a line from three watermelons to the number three.

"Maybe if you tell me . . ."

"Maxine . . ." Wat started to plead.

"Are you afraid something bad is going to happen?"

"I don't know," Wat insisted.

"Did Dr. Stone—"

"I don't know!"

"Maxine," Toni interrupted, "you don't give up, do you?"

"What do you mean?" Maxine asked.

"Like Seligman."

Maxine sat up. "What do you mean, like Seligman?"

"With the contest, with getting me to be your partner."

"Then you'll do it?" Maxine asked. "You'll do it?"

"I still don't know," Toni said, filling in another answer.

"I don't think it'll be hard tutoring him," Maxine argued.

"I don't know," Toni repeated, watching Wat. He had slid away into a corner by the bed, as far away from her as he could get.

"But didn't you say you had a special invention idea for your grandmother?" Maxine asked.

"I don't know."

"But what don't you know?" Maxine asked.

"I don't know what I don't know," Toni said, shrugging. She looked down at her book at the next problem. Maxine watched Toni read the problem to herself, pause a few seconds, then write down the answer in her loose-leaf notebook. They were complicated multiplication problems, long, twisted puzzles, all these cars going in different directions on different days at different speeds. "A car leaves Texas and drives to Chicago," Maxine reread. Her mind wasn't working. She glanced at Toni's book. Toni was already up to problem six. She turned to her brother. Wat drew a red line from the word *six* to a picture of six oranges.

"Wat," she said, suddenly angry, "you're not supposed to be able to read. How come you can read the word *six*, but you can't write it?"

"I don't know," he said, and traced a line from a picture of eight bananas to the word *eight*.

Maxine slid over to him. He had connected nine birds to the word *nine*. He had also drawn a line from a picture of twelve pink frogs to the word *twelve*.

"Hey! How come you can read those words, but you can't write them?"

"I don't know," he said, ignoring her anger. He connected three green horses to the word *three*.

She stood up. She wanted to jump out her window. She looked at the clock above her desk. It was four-thirty. Phil would be on in another half hour. His guests were supposed to be parents who claimed their children were aliens from other galaxies. Looking down at Toni and Wat at work, silently, effortlessly, Maxine wondered if possibly, just possibly, Toni and Wat could be from another planet. Both of them seemed to have secrets. Neither of them was sure of anything. Except for saying yes to her invitation to come over and do her homework, Toni hadn't really said anything other than "I don't know" all afternoon. Maxine had asked her about tutoring Victor, about the invention contest, and about what Toni's grandmother thought when Toni told her where she was spending the afternoon.

"I don't know" had been Toni's answer to every question.

"But when you talked to her this morning and you told her you were going to my house to do your homework and talk about your invention ideas, how did she sound?"

"I don't know."

And Wat. He wasn't sure of anything.

"Wat," she said, testing him, "when you drink milk,

what do you like better, your flavor straw or your Crazy Straw?"

"I don't know," Wat told her, coloring a zebra pink and green.

Maybe, Maxine reasoned, maybe Wat and Toni were aliens. And maybe neither of them had been told all the correct answers to all the questions earthlings ask.

"Toni," she said, trying to sound mildly curious, "what hospital were you born in?"

Toni stopped writing. She rubbed her nose with her pencil eraser. "You know," she said, thinking about it, "I don't know."

"Oh," Maxine said, trying to sound as if she didn't care.

Toni's an alien, she told herself. Toni's an alien, and either she doesn't remember what they told her to say before they landed her, or they just didn't know that much about the earth. Maybe that's why she's here. She's supposed to find out things. Maybe that's why she's in my class. Maybe the aliens know about me, about all that stuff I've almost invented. Maybe they've been watching me. Maybe I'm almost famous on another planet.

But what about Wat?

"Wat," she said, again trying to sound bored, mildly curious. "How many millions of miles are we from the sun?"

"Me and you, Maxine?" Wat asked.

"Everybody, the whole *planet.*" She stressed the word *planet.*

"I don't know," he told her.

He's just pretending he doesn't know, Maxine assured herself. The aliens probably instructed him to pretend to know nothing. They probably weren't sure what a five-year-old earthling was supposed to know. She ran down the evidence against Wat. He says he can't read, but he can read numbers. He can read, but he can't write. He knows the names of every dinosaur, but he can't tie his shoe. He talks to his stuffed animals. He's an alien.

It was too much. She jumped to her feet. "How come," she challenged Toni and Wat, "how come all the two of you ever say is, 'I don't know'?" She was serious. If they were aliens, she wanted to know why she was already famous on another planet while her own planet, the entire planet, was still ignoring her.

Toni sat up and leaned against Maxine's bureau. "How come," Toni asked, "you never say 'I don't know'?"

"Yeah, Maxine," Wat said, also sitting up. He slid closer to Toni. "How come you always know everything? How come?"

"I have to," Maxine said, sitting on her bed. She reached over and grabbed Lorenzo, her stuffed dragon. She hugged him to her chest.

"You have to?" Toni asked, openly doubting her.

"Yes," Maxine informed her.

"Why?" Toni asked in disbelief.

"Because I'm going to be on Phil's show," Maxine patiently explained. "And you can't say 'I don't know' on Phil's show. Nobody applauds. You have to have all the answers."

"But you're only ten years old!" Toni laughed.

"I'm almost eleven," Maxine pointed out. "And if you say you'll tutor Victor, you'll be on Phil's show too. Then we'll both have to answer questions from his studio audience and his viewers at home."

"Well, there's not going to be a lot of applause, let me tell you, Maxine, because there's a lot I don't know. A real lot."

"So then I'll take the questions."

"Wait." Toni waved her hands, laughing. "So if you get on Phil's show, no matter what anybody asks you, you're going to be able to give them an answer?"

"I'll have to," Maxine admitted.

"But what if . . ." Toni wondered out loud, "what if somebody calls you on the show and asks you . . . how come . . . how come the hair on your head keeps growing, but the hair on your eyebrows doesn't? What are you going to say?"

"I'm an inventor," Maxine argued. "Why is somebody going to ask me that?"

"I don't know," Toni said, holding out her hands, obviously enjoying herself. "People from all over the country will be watching. Maybe that's the kind of thing they worry about in . . . in Cleveland. 'Hello,' "

Toni said, picking up an imaginary phone. She tried to make her voice sound like an old man's. " 'I'm from Cleveland, and I was just wonderin', how come the hair on my head keeps growin', but the hair on my eyebrows don't?' "

"Yeah, how come?" Wat asked.

"Because," Maxine said, rubbing her chin and gazing up at the ceiling, "because . . . because . . . because your eyebrow hairs are glued in tighter."

Toni clapped her hands and shrieked, "That's what you're going to say on national television?"

"There's no glue behind your face!" Wat laughed.

"So? It's an answer. It's as good as any other answer," Maxine said confidently. "Go ahead, ask me another."

"How come, how come," Wat asked, standing up and walking around in a small circle, "how come you never see any baby pigeons?"

"That's easy," Maxine said, leaning back against the wall behind her bed. "That's because . . . that's because sparrows are really baby pigeons."

"That's not true!" Wat complained.

"So?" Maxine said. "I made it up. It should be true. Ask me another."

Wat sat down. In Toni's lap. Toni brushed his long blond hair with her fingers. He looked like her doll.

"You want another question?" Toni asked her.

"From our studio audience, or our viewers at home."

"I can't think of anything," Toni admitted.

"Next caller, please!"

Suddenly the room became quiet. Maxine pulled her legs up to her chest and wrapped her arms around them. Toni put her arms around Wat. She stopped smiling. Her eyes were open in wonder. "What happens," she asked Maxine, "what happens to our old words after we say them? Where do they go?"

"I don't know," Maxine admitted.

"You think," Toni said, "you think they just fall and sort of melt into the ground like snow? Or do you think they float out into space? You think space is filled with all of our old sounds?"

Maxine didn't know what to say.

"Ha!" Toni laughed. "I got you there! Caught you without an answer."

"So you'll tutor Victor?" Maxine asked, changing the subject.

"What happens if I don't?"

"Mr. Seligman told me if he agreed to the contest, I should encourage you to do it."

"If I don't tutor Victor, he won't let us have the contest?"

"He doesn't want to write to your grandmother, Toni. He doesn't want to get you in any more trouble. I heard him talking to Mrs. Krill. He thinks you're special. I think he wants you to prove something to him. Tutor Victor. It can't be that hard."

Toni sighed. She slid Wat off her lap, gathered her books, and stood up. "I'd better get going," she said. "I have to go do things at home."

"So?" Maxine asked, standing also. She squeezed Toni's hand. "We'll start working on the contest tomorrow?"

"Maxine," Toni said, pulling her hand away. She looked behind her at Maxine's door. "Didn't anybody warn you about me?"

Maxine nodded. "A few people," she admitted. "So? We'll start tomorrow, okay? We can work on that idea you said you had for your grandmother."

"You know, Maxine, all the kids I hung around with last year, their mothers told them to stay away from me."

"They weren't inventors," Maxine said.

"So?" Toni shrugged. "So I guess we'll start tomorrow."

Standing at her front door, the afternoon sun slanting low into her eyes, Maxine squinted as she watched Toni walk quickly away up the block. Wat stood by her side.

"She's nice," Wat said.

"Maxine?" her father asked.

She turned around.

Her father's hands were in his pockets. He took a deep breath and smiled. He looked tired. He laughed. "I would like to put in a request. For an invention."

# 11

# No

*October 5*

From across the cafeteria, Maxine watched Toni try to convince Victor to accept her tutoring. Seated by himself at the end of the boys' table, dressed in his camouflage shirt and pants, Victor shook his head. He didn't want Toni to tutor him. Toni waved her arms. She pointed a finger at Victor's nose. Victor shrank into his shoulders.

"Just don't hit him," Maxine wished out loud. She returned to her lunch invention. She had hollowed out the core of an apple and stuffed its insides with peanut butter, chocolate chips, and raisins. Then she had replaced the top of the apple. This way, nobody knew that her simple, dull apple contained an entire meal and dessert.

She had disguised her meal because lately, somebody was stealing her lunch. Who? She snuck a bite of her apple, then looked about the cafeteria at the kids around her. Everyone sat in pairs or small groups, chatting or playing. Some of the girls had out their dolls or games. Some boys were bunched together at the end of their table, copying drawings from comic books. Hector and Luis smashed their G.I. Joes into each other and screamed "Pow!" and "Bam!" Patti and Asali stood behind Orlando, making grotesque faces at each other. The cafeteria was noisy with laughter.

Who was picking on her? Before she became friends with Toni, nobody knew she even existed.

The whistle blew. Recess.

Mayhem. Kids leapt to their feet, howling and hooting. Derek and Pete slid their food trays across the table into the already overstuffed garbage, scattering food all over the floor. Mr. Vim, the lunchroom monitor, shrieked, "Pick that up, fellows!"

Maxine ducked to avoid flying milk containers. One exploded on the wall behind her.

"Be orderly! Be orderly!" Mr. Vim shouted, stamping his foot.

Two hundred children rushed at the exits to the yard. Maxine held her breath and looked the other way. She didn't want to see anybody trampled to death.

"He's still afraid of me," Toni complained, returning to Maxine. She punched her fist into her hand. "He makes me furious!"

"What did you say to him?"

"I told him if he keeps telling me I scare him, I'm going to hit him."

"I bet that really calmed him down," Maxine said.

Toni sat beside her and laughed. "I was kidding, I was kidding! I told him I'd tutor him in math. I told him if he let me, I'd help him pass this year."

"What did he say?"

"He said, 'Go away.' He said that a lot. I said, 'Hello, Victor.' He said, 'Go away, Toni.' I said, 'You want me to help you pass math this year?' He said, 'Go away.' Then the whistle blew, and he went away."

"How come he's so frightened of you?"

"Something from last year," Toni said, looking up at the clock on the wall. It was spattered with milk. "Something happened." She looked back down at the table, then up at Maxine. "Everybody's afraid of me. I guess I'm not a nice kid, Maxine. You just haven't learned that yet." She grabbed Maxine's apple out of her hands and took a bite. "Hey!" she cried. "What's this?" She removed the lid of the apple and peered into its core.

"My lunch kept disappearing," Maxine said. "I invented something."

"You invented an apple?" Toni joked.

"No, it's a lunch invention. It's a secret lunch. It's a whole meal inside an apple."

"It's delicious!" Toni took another bite. "You know," she teasingly confided in Maxine, "there's peanut butter in there. And raisins. You know that?" She dipped her finger into the well of the apple and scooped up a dab of peanut butter. She licked her finger. "This is a great idea, Maxine."

"How come people keep stealing my lunch?" she asked.

"Because nobody likes us," Toni said matter-of-factly. "You know, this apple is clever. You don't need bread. You don't need tinfoil, or even a little plastic bag. It's not going to pollute anything. And it's cheap. It's a great idea."

"Why doesn't anybody like us?" Maxine asked.

"Because you're too strange, and because I'm not nice," Toni said. "I spoke to Mr. Seligman before. He said I don't have to tutor Victor if I don't want to."

"So why do you keep trying?"

"Because when Mr. Seligman sees my grandmother, he'll say, 'I gave Toni a chance, Mrs. Skye. I gave her plenty of chances.' And my grandmother will think everything is just the same all over again. I'm messing up." She swiveled on her seat and watched Victor walk out of the cafeteria by himself. He stared at the ground while he walked. He was wearing black combat boots.

"Everybody's just waiting for me to blow it," she said, glaring at Victor.

"But if you tutor Victor," Maxine said hopefully, "and we enter the contest—"

"What am I going to do in the contest?" Toni asked bitterly, turning to face Maxine. "I don't have any invention ideas, Maxine. I don't. I said I did, but I don't. I've never even had one idea!" Toni put down the apple. She rubbed her lips with her fist.

"My father gave me an idea," Maxine said.

Toni rolled her eyes, as if Maxine were telling a bad joke.

Maxine told Toni about Wat—about the murmur, about the tiny hole in his heart.

"But he's so little," Toni argued.

"He was born with it," Maxine explained.

"He's going to be all right, though, isn't he?" Toni asked, looking worried.

"They just need to watch it," Maxine explained. "They use this machine called an echocardiograph that looks at Wat's heart. But Wat won't lie still for it. He gets too scared. So my father asked if we could invent something for Wat that he could take with him into the examination, something to make him not so scared."

"Wat and my *grandmother*. My grandmother is scared of everything. She won't go out. She won't sleep," Toni said.

"Maybe we could invent something for your grandmother, too," Maxine suggested.

Toni pushed up her glasses and rubbed her eyes. Absentmindedly, she took another bite of the apple.

"What happened to your lunch?" Maxine asked, standing and putting on her jacket.

Embarrassed, Toni put down the apple. "Sorry." She slid the apple back to Maxine.

"No." Maxine waved away Toni's apology. "You can have it."

"I could get the free lunch," Toni explained, "but she won't fill out the forms. She said she's too proud."

"Finish it. That's the second one," Maxine lied. "I ate the first one when you were talking to Victor." She backed away toward the door. "I'm going to go talk to him."

"Maxine," Toni called. "Don't listen to what anybody else says about me."

"Sure," Maxine agreed. "You know," she said, "nobody's ever asked me to invent something before. You should start thinking of some ideas while I talk to Victor. We're running out of time."

# 12

# Victor

## A Few Minutes Later

V ictor wasn't easy to find. He wasn't with any of the groups of children who were playing in the yard. Though Maxine hardly knew him, she thought he seemed suspicious of just about everybody. She knew he liked to keep to himself, and she wondered about him—about his camouflage suit, the military magazines everybody said he kept in his desk, and his bags of toy soldiers that he was always carrying around. He was so small and quiet, yet he seemed to have a little war going on inside his head.

She found him kneeling on the ground in a sunny spot at the back of the yard. He was drawing a picture of a tank on the black pavement. He had worn his chalk down to a piece no bigger than his thumbnail.

"You know," Maxine said, trying to sound friendly, "I invented . . . I almost invented a chalk that sparkles."

Victor continued drawing, ignoring her. Maxine admired his work. His tank seemed almost real. The tank's treads appeared to rise off the pavement.

"I made it by combining chalk dust, the powder from some match heads, and the scrapings from my sparklers from the Fourth of July," she explained.

Victor looked up. "That's in July, right?"

"What is?" Maxine asked.

"The Fourth of July," he said. "That's in July, right?"

"Of course it is," Maxine said, looking back to the cafeteria. "Why do you think they call it the Fourth of July?"

"I don't know," Victor said, returning to his drawing. He was working on the tank's cannon. "Boom!" he said, and drew a puff of smoke billowing from the mouth of the gun. He stood up to review his work.

"What do you mean, you don't know?" Maxine asked.

"I just thought it was its name," he said, squinting at her, as if she were too bright to face. "Like Halloween. That's just its name, and that happens in October, right?"

"Right," Maxine said.

"So you can give me some fireworks?" Victor asked.

"Fireworks? I don't have any fireworks. I have chalk. I almost invented a chalk that sparkles when you write with it."

"You don't have any fireworks?"

"I have chalk. I have chalk that sparkles."

"You don't have those kind of fireworks that are shaped like pineapples that G.I. Joe throws over his shoulder, do you?"

"Hand grenades?"

"Yeah, that's them," Victor said eagerly.

"Victor," Maxine said, becoming angry. "I have a piece of chalk that maybe sparkles when you write with it."

"I was just asking," Victor said apologetically. "I was just asking. I didn't really want a hand grenade. I mean, if you had one . . ." Victor stopped talking. He was looking behind Maxine.

She turned around. Toni had stepped out of the cafeteria and was leaning against the school building, her arms folded.

"You know," Victor said, pointing his thumb at Toni, "she's dangerous."

"She's *dangerous*?" Maxine asked in disbelief.

"You should have seen her last year. She was bad. Everybody was afraid of her."

"Well, she's different this year," Maxine insisted.

"But she was different last year, too. All the time. Sometimes she was friendly. And sometimes you just said the wrong thing and she'd go crazy. She'd explode."

Maxine glanced back at the cafeteria and waved hello to Toni. Toni waved back.

"You should have seen her with her friends. They stole. They beat up kids. They busted all of the girls' toilets on the third floor. We had Mrs. Jacobson last year. She was afraid of Toni. When she'd ask Toni to do something, Toni would just say no. She was scary."

"But this year—" Maxine started to say.

"That's why her mother gave her up," Victor said.

Maxine lost her breath. Her face felt hot. It was burning. "Her mother gave her up?"

"Yeah, that's what everybody says. That's what I heard. That's why she's with her grandmother. 'Cause her mother just left."

Toni was still standing there by the door, waiting. Maxine knew Toni had finally begun to believe in her. Even rely on her. Toni had begun to treat her like a friend.

"Victor," Maxine said, stepping closer to him and lowering her voice. "Toni's going to tutor you."

"No, she's not. I don't want her to."

"Well, she is," Maxine said. "You need the tutoring. You know you won't pass if she doesn't help you."

"She'll kill me if I make a mistake."

"How about I give you something to protect yourself?"

"You have bullets?" Victor asked excitedly.

"What? Bullets? You have a gun?"

"No!" Victor laughed nervously, waving his hands, as if he were cleaning the air of the word.

"Then what are you going to do with bullets?"

"Throw them at her?" he asked.

"What?"

"Only if she threatens me," he added.

"How about I give you my chalk?" Maxine said, quickly glancing back at Toni, who was now holding her hands up in the air, as if to ask what was happening.

"How's that going to protect me?" Victor asked.

"It sparkles," Maxine assured him. "It sparkles. Toni's afraid of anything that sparkles."

"That's true?"

"It's true," Maxine reassured him. "So?"

"She's really good at math, you know," Victor told her.

"I know she is," Maxine said. "I'll tell her you said yes."

The whistle blew. Recess was over.

# ☆ 13 ☆

# Bad Dreams

### October 7

"Your brother"—Toni smiled proudly, returning to the kitchen—"is asleep."

"We're in trouble," Maxine said, looking up from her inventor's journal. She had been keeping the notebook since she was seven. There was nothing in it that could make Wat less scared. "We have eight days until the deadline."

"Well, that was fun," Toni said, pulling out a chair. "I read him *The Prince of Horses.* As soon as I finished reading, he fell asleep. Maxine, Wat doesn't know he's got a hole in his heart?"

"He doesn't understand it. My father tells him the murmur is just a funny sound his heart makes. That everybody's heart plays some kind of song, and his song is special."

"I like that," Toni said. She leaned over the table and glanced at Maxine's notes. "I sat there and watched him sleeping for a minute. It was nice."

"You should see him at nap time at school," Maxine said, quickly turning to a blank page. Her notes were too embarrassing—one failure after another. "He's a terror. He's driving that teacher crazy. He won't nap, and he's gotten the other kids not to nap."

"What do they do?"

"I asked him. He said they just sit there and watch each other until Mrs. Finch starts yelling at them to close their eyes and go to sleep."

Toni laughed and slid back into her chair. Maxine rose and went to the refrigerator. She poured two glasses of milk and removed a package of cookies from an overstuffed cabinet. "I think Wat likes you," Maxine said, bringing the milk and cookies over to the table.

"I think he trusts me," Toni said, opening up the Inventions of Children Contest manual. She read aloud from the first page: " 'Before you sit down to create something new, ask yourself what your everyday problems are. Study how they are solved.' So, Maxine, what are your everyday problems?"

"My brother gets scared when people look at his heart."

"That's not really an everyday problem," Toni said.

"I'm not famous," Maxine said. "Nobody's ever heard of me. That's an everyday problem."

"I think they're looking for something smaller."

"That's my smallest problem. I don't have anything smaller. All I think about is Wat. How about you? What are your everyday problems?"

"Victor," Toni said, taking a handful of cookies from the bag. She placed them in a neat pile by her glass. "Victor! Our first day of tutoring, he wears a football helmet! In the library! He just sits down with this helmet on. I said, 'Victor, take off your helmet.' He said, 'No.' I thought he was kidding. I tried to make a joke out of it. I said, 'Victor, when Maxine said I could help you pass, this is not what she meant.' He didn't laugh. So I said, 'Victor, if you don't take off your helmet, I'm going to unscrew your head.' "

"What did he say to that?" Maxine asked, dipping a cookie into her milk. The cookie fell apart.

"He said, 'See! That's why I'm wearing a helmet!' "

"Did you tutor him?"

"Yeah, but it was hard," Toni admitted. "He couldn't see the paper because of all those bars crisscrossing his face. I had to rap out the numbers on the top of his helmet." She sipped some milk. "Victor, *he's* my problem."

Maxine leaned over the table and took the contest manual from Toni. "It says here, 'Think of problems a machine could solve.' "

Toni shrugged. She was lost. Maxine wrote IDEAS on the top of a page. She numbered the page from one to twenty. "Ideas," she said aloud. "You don't have any other problems? One that a machine could solve?"

"How come," Toni asked, "Wat won't nap in school?"

"Bad dreams," Maxine said, looking down at her

blank page. "He's afraid if he closes his eyes, he'll get bad dreams. Maybe that's why he won't close his eyes during his heart exam. He's afraid of getting bad dreams."

"That's strange. So is my grandmother. That's why she won't sleep at night. She's like those kids in Wat's class. She just sits up on the couch and stares. She says when it's dark and quiet, she starts to think about my mother."

"What happened to your mother?"

"I don't know," Toni said, looking down into her milk. "My grandma doesn't know what happened to my mother, either. She says at night, she starts thinking about it, and everything becomes too sad and frightening for her to sleep. She says she can only sleep in the daytime. She says she needs the noise."

"Maybe," Maxine said, suddenly excited, "maybe we could make an invention that prevents bad dreams." In her notebook under IDEAS, she hurriedly wrote, *Bad dreams*.

"And we can make everything go backward," Toni said, dismissing the thought. "And we can make a machine that would send my mother flying backward into my window just to ask what I was wearing to school that morning."

"But—" Maxine started to apologize.

"Maybe you should do what your father asked," Toni said. She stood up and pushed in her chair. "I forgot," she said quietly. "I have to get home." She picked up her backpack from the floor and slung it over her shoulder.

"I thought you were going to stay for dinner," Maxine said.

"I can't," Toni said, walking through the living room to the front door. "My grandmother will forget to eat. She'll forget to cook. She'll just forget."

Maxine watched Toni shrug and pull the door closed behind her.

## ☆ 14 ☆

# Trust

*October 8*

Maxine waited for Victor to leave the library. It was three-thirty. All the other kids had gone home. From the hallway, she watched Toni point out a trick for Victor to learn how to multiply by fives. "Just take half the number and add a zero," she said.

Victor nodded.

He wasn't wearing a helmet.

"Six times five," Toni said, writing on his paper. "Half of six is three. Six times five is thirty. Eighteen times five. Half of eighteen is nine. Eighteen times five is ninety."

Victor nodded.

"Then how come you're not writing any of this down?" Toni asked.

Victor smiled and held up the stub of a pencil. "No point," he said.

Maxine could see Toni look up at the clock inside the library. "All this time," she asked, sounding frustrated, "your pencil didn't have a point?"

"Nope," Victor cheerfully admitted.

"You think you'll remember anything I told you?" Toni asked.

"Nope." He offered Toni a smile. "Am I done for today?"

"I guess," Toni said, looking down at her own open loose-leaf notebook.

Maxine watched Victor stuff his books into his green camouflage backpack. She watched him put on his green camouflage cap.

"Victor," Toni asked. "Why do you dress that way?"

"Camouflage," Victor told her, walking toward the door.

"Camouflage?" Toni repeated. "Who are you hiding from?"

He wouldn't say. Maxine stepped aside to let him out of the library. She watched him disappear into the stairwell at the end of the hall. She glanced down at the Inventions of Children Contest manual in her hands.

"It says here," she announced, entering the library, waving the manual like a flag, "that we're supposed to be creative. We're supposed to put all our ideas down on paper. It says, 'Let your imagination run wild.' That's what it says."

"Hello, Maxine," Toni said.

Maxine sat down in Victor's old seat. She removed her clipboard and placed it on the table opposite Toni's loose-leaf notebook.

"So," she asked Toni, trying to show as much enthusiasm as possible. "So what causes bad dreams?"

"Victor," Toni said, closing her loose-leaf notebook. "Victor causes bad dreams. I'm teaching him how to multiply by nine. He says, 'You know they invented a plane that's almost invisible? Enemy radar can't find it.' I say, 'You worried about enemy radar, Victor?' He says, 'Sometimes.' I think Victor wants to be the Invisible Man when he grows up."

Toni took the manual from Maxine and spun it around. "You know, I'm almost starting to feel sorry for him."

"How come?"

"I don't know. What do you think he's hiding from?"

Maxine shrugged.

"I want to help him," Toni said, sounding as if she surprised herself. "I want to help him pass."

"I don't think that's going to be too easy," Maxine reminded her.

"And inventing a machine that gets rid of bad dreams is?"

"Listen," Maxine urged. "Let's just think about bad dreams. Then we'll make a list. On one side, we'll write down what causes them. On the other side, we'll write down possible solutions. Maybe we'll come up with something."

"I don't have any ideas, Maxine," Toni insisted.

"Your grandmother gets bad dreams. My brother

gets bad dreams. We don't want them to have bad dreams anymore," Maxine said.

"Maxine, what if I don't want to become famous?"

"Don't worry about it," Maxine assured her. "When we're on Phil's show, I'll do all the talking."

"Where's Wat?" Toni asked.

"He's with some after-school program in the auditorium. They're teaching him about computers and how to make sock puppets."

Toni laughed.

Maxine removed a piece of lined paper from her clipboard and folded it vertically. On the top of the left column she wrote, *Causes bad dreams*. On the top of the right column she wrote, *Solves bad dreams*. She numbered both sides, from one to twenty.

"Your grandmother," Maxine said. "I promised her we were going to win it. And now I have to do something for Wat. I have to."

Toni leaned over and read Maxine's writing upside down. "Causes bad dreams? My grandmother says it's too quiet when she lies down at night."

Maxine rubbed her chin with the eraser on her pencil. She considered the problem.

"How about," Toni said jokingly, "a machine that makes noise?"

Maxine wrote it down.

"What else?" she asked Toni. "What else keeps her awake?"

"She says she feels too alone at night."

Maxine wrote the problem down in the left column.

"And how about," Toni said, again joking, "a machine that provides her with company?"

Maxine looked up at Toni, smiled, and then wrote down her idea, word for word, in the right column. "Good thinking," she said as she wrote. "We have to be creative."

"I was kidding!"

"So?"

"So what are we going to do? Make a noisy machine that pops out people like a toaster?"

"That's not possible."

"So what are you doing?" Toni said, standing.

"Writing down ideas," Maxine said calmly.

"But they're not possible!"

"That doesn't mean we can't think about them," Maxine explained. "We might come up with something. Something that's almost possible. Something that's almost possible, but not impossible."

"You're crazy!" Toni said, sitting. "You don't give up!"

"I can't give up," Maxine explained. "It's supposed to be hard. If it was easy, somebody would have already invented it."

"Maxine, don't you think if there was some way to stop bad dreams, somebody would have discovered it? You think the answer has been waiting for us to come around?"

"Maybe," Maxine guessed. "Maybe it's ready for us."

Toni was exasperated. She gave in. "What gives your brother bad dreams?"

"In school?" Maxine asked. "In the daytime? I think he'll only lie down and close his eyes if he knows he's near somebody he trusts. I think that's what happens to him at Dr. Stone's office, too."

"So why don't you write that down?" Toni asked. "And then you could write down on the other side, 'A machine that creates trust.' " She stood and pushed in her chair.

"Where are you going?"

"Maxine," Toni said, packing up her books. "You don't understand. My grandmother won't eat until I get back. She won't sleep. She won't take care of herself. She won't move from that couch. She'll just sit there, wondering what kind of trouble I'm getting myself into. She won't breathe without me being there." She zipped her book bag shut.

"She almost sounds like Wat."

Toni took a step toward the door, then whirled around. "How?" she asked angrily. "Wat is five years old! How is my grandmother anything like your brother?"

"Because they're both stuck sitting up, scared?" Maxine wondered. "And they both need somebody to help them get unstuck?"

"Maxine," Toni cried, "she's a grown-up! I'm just a kid! What can I do? I'm just a kid!"

Clumsily, Maxine reached out to hug Toni, but Toni spun away and ran out of the library.

Maxine Candle
34-37 59th Drive
Woodside, Queens
New York, NY 11377

October 13

Phil Donahue
NBC
30 Rockefeller Center
New York, NY 10112

Dear Phil,

Let's say—now, I'm not saying this happened—but let's say my inventing partner disappeared for three days, and she didn't have a phone, and I couldn't call her, and I was kind of too uncomfortable just showing up at her apartment. And let's just say that before she disappeared, we were about to come up with an amazing invention idea.

If we missed the deadline for the contest, could we still be on your show?

The contest doesn't even matter anymore, if you want to know the truth. The invention does. It's going to be an important invention. People are going to want to know about it.

We would still have interesting things to say to your studio audience and your viewers at home. But the important thing would be the invention.

Let me tell you about it.

But first, don't let your secretary read this. I know she's been keeping my letters from you. I know she's reading this right now and thinking how she's going to explain to you that my letter wasn't important, and you don't have to read it. That's the reason I wrote on this envelope, "For Phil, not for his secretary."

Phil! Don't even open this envelope near her. Grab it and run into your office.

Wait. Don't run.

Phil, I just realized something.

If your secretary reads all of your letters, she's reading this, and I'm really talking to her and not to you.

All this time I've been talking to her and not to you.

Did you even read my first letter?

Who sent me the application for the contest?

Do you know I exist, Phil?

You don't know that I even exist.

Wait. I'll be right back. I have to talk to your secretary.

Even though you're not reading this,
Yours truly,

Maxine Candle

Maxine Candle
34-37 59th Drive
Woodside, Queens
New York, NY 11377

October 13
Phil Donahue's Secretary
NBC
30 Rockefeller Center
New York, NY 10112

Dear Phil Donahue's Secretary,
Look at me. Ever since I can remember, I've wanted to invent something, something that could help my brother, Wat. Wat was born with a heart murmur. I wanted to invent a machine that would keep him all right, or make him happier, or make things easier for him. I wanted to fix him up.

All right, so maybe I also wanted to become famous. Maybe I wanted to be on the "Donahue" show and tell everybody about my life and what I think, and show off my ideas. You see, Mrs. Phil Donahue's Secretary, I felt almost invisible, thinking about Wat all the time, and inventions, and nobody really thinking about me. If I got to be on the "Donahue" show, I thought, and 250 million people saw me, and asked me questions, and talked about me, I wouldn't be so invisible, would I?

That's why I wanted to be an inventor. And if everyone who watched Phil's show thought I was an inventor, then I really would be one, wouldn't I?

Maybe I was just using Wat as an excuse. Maybe I just wanted to make something that never existed before, something new.

Things have changed a little. My father asked me to invent something for Wat that would keep him calm during his heart exam. Before he asked me, my father used to think my inventions were cute. My mother thought they made Wat *more* worried. Now they need me!

And maybe also I wanted to do something for Toni, my invention partner. She's not a happy person. Maybe I wanted to invent something that could make her happy.

But maybe things haven't changed so much. This invention will do something. It will be like the birthday present everybody's always waiting for. It is too important. I need to invent it. It needs me to invent it. But we're going to miss the deadline. We're so close. We're almost there. We just about have the idea. But we're not going to be able to enter the contest.

Can't you wait for us? Can't you just wait for us to make our invention, then have us on your show?

Why did you send me that application? It

got me started on something. It got me to believe that people were waiting for me. It got me to believe I was becoming somebody.

Sincerely,

Maxine Candle

# ☆ 15 ☆

# The Phone Call

## *Early the Next Morning*

When the phone rang by her bed, Maxine sat up and looked at the clock. It was three in the morning. She smiled. It made perfect sense. Phil's secretary had read her letter. Now she was calling to tell her Phil would wait. He wanted her on the show. He wanted that invention.

Maxine had mailed the letter earlier that evening, right after another quiet dinner with neither of her parents talking much. Just, "How was school today? Did you get any homework?"

That was quick. Maxine guessed the post office rushed all of Phil's mail. Maybe the mailman had seen her running to the box?

It didn't matter. This was it. This was the phone call. She was going to be a famous inventor. They were waiting for her. She picked up the phone.

"I was wondering when you were going to pick up."

"Hello?"

"Just tell me. Just tell me. Do we have to build it? Do we have to build it, or do we just have to hand in the plans?"

The voice didn't sound the way Maxine had expected Phil's secretary to sound. It was too young and scratchy, and frantic.

"For the show?" Maxine asked.

"For the contest! Do we have to build the thing? I mean, I got it! She fell asleep in front of the television tonight. She's on cough medicine, and it knocked her out. And I got it!"

"*Toni?*"

"I ran downstairs to the pay phone to call you. I'm on my corner at the pay phone. I was just watching her, and I got it. It's a pillow! A soft pillow. Maybe it's got some sweet-smelling perfume in it, like flowers. And inside the pillow, there are voices of people you know, people you trust."

"Where have you been?" Maxine asked, sitting up in her bed.

"Home. She's been sick. I had to take her to the clinic. She's got the flu. Then it became bronchitis. She's going to be all right now. I just had to stay home and take care of her. Listen. It's got voices!"

"The pillow?" Maxine asked, lowering her voice. She didn't want to wake up Wat.

"Yeah. Inside it. But they're soft. And they sound near, maybe like in another room. They're voices you trust."

"They're on tape?"

"Yes! Company. They're company. And some friendly noise. And trust. And you can almost hear them laughing, or saying your name, or telling a funny story you sort of remember, and it just plays on and on and on, until you're asleep. Do we have to build it?"

"We have to display a working model of it on Thursday. They judge the model. That's what they vote on to pick the winner."

"Thursday? What's today?"

"Tuesday."

"Tuesday? I've been out three days?"

"I was worried."

"Three days?"

Maxine could hear strange, sharp sounds in the background. Something screeching. A car's horn.

"Maxine. Can you build it?"

"Of course I can build it," she said, sliding her feet into her slippers. Her father's toolbox was under the sink. The phone-answering machine was on the dining-room table. She would have to take out the tape. It was a continuous loop. In a regular tape player, it would continue to play its thirty-second message until somebody shut it off.

"You can build the whole thing?"

"I can build it," Maxine promised, "but I just realized something. We have to test it. We have to hand in our test results to Mr. Seligman by tomorrow afternoon. How are we going to get to your grandmother by then?"

"Test it on Wat," Toni said.

"Can you be in school tomorrow?" Maxine asked. "I'll bring it."

"I'll be there. You think we'll win?"

"Of course we'll win." Maxine laughed. She would use the tape player from the inside of her old Chatty Betty doll. Betty spoke when you hugged her. She would put that device inside the pillow. When you hugged it, it would speak.

"Maxine," Toni said excitedly, "if she sleeps at night, she could start going out again. You can do that? You can make it work?"

The phone suddenly filled with static.

"Please deposit twenty-five cents for the next five minutes."

"I can show her the award!" Toni shouted over the static. More traffic sounds squealed and wailed in the background. "We get an award, right? We win something she could hang up?"

"She can watch us on Phil's show," Maxine said, wondering where she had buried her old dolls.

"Please deposit twenty-five cents."

"Oh, no!" Toni shrieked. "I'm wearing my pajamas!"

"Please deposit . . ."

Maxine listened to the phone line die. She hung up the receiver and put on her robe.

"Some friendly noise," she said to herself. "And voices."

# ☆ 16 ☆

# It Works!

## October 15

"What if she's really a police lady?" Wat asked as they approached the school. He was wearing his bright yellow slicker. Maxine walked along, quietly holding her big pillow, covered in plastic, in her arms. She searched the playground for Toni. It was before eight, but the yard was already filled with kids, many of them also dressed in bright, slick red or yellow raincoats. It was a cool, damp morning, and limp brown leaves were scattered about the ground everywhere.

"Where's Toni?" Maxine asked, pulling open the gate and walking down the steps into the yard. Her pillow scratched her nose. Through a small hole in the plastic, she could smell peaches and cinnamon. Early in the morning, she had gathered up the potpourri sachets in her drawers and emptied them into the pillowcase.

The yard was filled with shadows. Everything was gray and wet.

"You think she'll arrest me?" Wat asked, tugging on Maxine's sleeve.

"Who?" Maxine said, watching two first graders throw handfuls of wet leaves at each other.

"Mrs. Benitez. She's going to be our new helper. Mrs. Finch said we're getting a new teacher-helper today. What if she's really a police lady?"

"Wat," Maxine said, "why would she be a police lady?"

"To arrest me?" Wat wondered.

"For not napping?" Maxine asked.

Wat nodded. "Mrs. Finch said Mrs. Fowler was right. It's the law. She said I'm making other kids break the law too. She could arrest me for that?"

"Wat," Maxine said, looking around for Toni, "you're not going to have any more nap problems."

"Oh, yes, I will."

"No, you won't," Maxine explained. "You'll put your head on this"—she showed him the pillow—"and you'll hear Mommy and Daddy talking. I recorded them this morning at breakfast. You'll put your head down, and it'll sound like they're just in the other room. And you can bring the pillow with you when you go to Dr. Stone for your echocardiogram. Whenever you close your eyes and put your head down, it'll be like you're at breakfast at home."

"What if she tries to put handcuffs on me?" Wat asked, ignoring Maxine. "What if she puts me in jail?"

"Hiya, Maxine."

It was Shawnna. Elisa, who was about half Shawnna's size, was standing by her side, almost as if they were attached.

"Look," Shawnna urged Maxine, holding up a piece of paper.

Maxine read the writing on the paper. "Elisa, I'll meet you in the yard at recess."

"Get it?" Shawnna asked. Elisa giggled.

"No," Maxine said, confused. "Why don't you just show it to Elisa yourself?"

Again Shawnna laughed. Elisa giggled.

"Look!" Shawnna thrust the paper right under Maxine's nose. Maxine stepped back and took the paper from Shawnna and examined it closely. The writing was in brown ink. It smelled of lemons.

"It's invisible ink!" Shawnna exclaimed.

Elisa giggled.

"No, it's not," Maxine said, giving Shawnna back her paper. "I can read it."

It began to drizzle.

"Put your hood on," Maxine told Wat.

Reluctantly, Wat put on his hood and pulled the drawstrings, cinching the hood so that it closed around his face, leaving only his nose sticking out.

"Maxine!" Shawnna laughed. "It was invisible. It was your ink, remember?"

"The one I invented?" Maxine guessed. "Out of milk and lemon juice?"

"This is what you wrote with it," Shawnna reminded her.

"It worked?" Maxine asked. "My invention worked?"

"No." Shawnna laughed. "When it was yours, it didn't work. It stayed invisible. But Elisa found out how to make it visible again."

"You hold it over a lamp," Elisa explained. "The heat makes the sugar in the lemons and milk turn brown."

"It worked?" Maxine was delighted. "Wat, it worked." She kicked Wat's foot.

"Is it still raining?" Wat asked from inside his hood.

"It worked!" she repeated. She had invented something that worked, that was useful. Somebody had come to her to thank her.

"Maxine," Shawnna said, "when you did it, it didn't work. But we fixed it. We're going to enter it in the Inventions of Children Contest."

"But it was my idea!"

"Almost." Shawnna giggled. "But not quite."

It began to pour.

Maxine took Wat's hand and ran inside.

The cafeteria smelled of two hundred wet raincoats and four hundred damp socks. Maxine stopped and stuck her nose into the small hole in the plastic bag surrounding her pillow. She breathed in deeply. Peaches and cinnamon. She looked up. The cafeteria was filled with kids who were laughing and screaming. The noise level was overwhelming: waves and waves of voices—arguing, shouting, joking. Everybody who had been playing in the yard had rushed in to join the kids who had come early for their free breakfasts.

"Look for Toni!" Maxine shouted into the small area of face she could see through Wat's hood. "We need her."

"Are we inside yet?" Wat yelled from inside his hood.

"We're in the cafeteria!" Maxine yelled back. "Just look for Toni!"

Wat turned his whole body to the left, then to the right.

"I can't see anything!" he yelled to Maxine.

"There she is!" Maxine announced. Tucking the pillow under her arm, she grabbed Wat's hand and led him to the back of the cafeteria.

Toni had been easy to spot. She was sitting with Victor. Surrounded by tables and tables of kids in bright yellow and red raincoats, Victor was wearing his dull green camouflage poncho. As Maxine and Wat approached, she could see Toni leaning over a book, explaining something to Victor.

"Elisa and Shawnna are using one of my ideas!" Maxine yelled.

Toni looked up. She noticed the pillow and smiled broadly. "You did it?" She stood and took the pillow from Maxine. "You made it?" she asked, excitedly removing the plastic.

"They're using my invisible ink for the invention contest!" Maxine complained.

"You have invisible ink?" Victor asked.

"I invented it!" Maxine yelled at him.

"Does it work?" Victor asked. "Can you send secret messages with it?"

Toni sat down and pressed her nose deep into the pillow. "It smells like fruit and flowers," she said with a laugh.

"I stuffed it with the potpourri from my underwear drawer," Maxine said, sitting on the bench next to Victor. She pulled Wat down beside her.

"I still can't see anything, Maxine!" Wat yelled.

Maxine leaned across Victor to Toni and pointed to a small $x$ on the pillow's sleeve. "Press your cheek against it."

Toni pressed her cheek against the pillow, turning on the tape player inside. Maxine watched Toni's eyes as Toni listened to the sounds of Maxine's parents preparing breakfast.

"You got the ink with you?" Victor asked Maxine.

Maxine ignored him. She watched Toni's eyes as Toni listened to Maxine's parents discuss their day.

"It works!" Toni declared. She grinned. She turned around and placed the pillow gently on top of the open book she had been using with Victor. She smoothed a crease in the pillowcase.

"You did it, Maxine. You did it."

Maxine suddenly felt like crying. She bit her lip.

"You know," Victor said, sticking his face inches away from Maxine's nose, "that kind of ink, invisible ink, is good in case you're ever captured . . ."

# ☆ 17 ☆

# And the Winner Is . . .

## A Few Minutes Later

There were seven volcanoes, many of them active. Shamel's was overflowing with pink lava. Miranda was having trouble with her baking soda and vinegar. Erik's volcano, which had miniature trees and a tiny village at its base, was hissing ominously.

"Volcanoes aren't inventions," Toni complained to Maxine.

"Unless you're going to get the volcano to do something for you, like heat water for tea, it's not an invention," Maxine agreed.

"That's a good idea." Toni smiled, hugging the pillow. "Using a whole volcano to make you a cup of tea."

"Those kids"—Maxine shook her head—"they hear the word *science* and they rush home and build stupid volcanoes. You didn't have to follow the rules. You didn't need a partner. Mr. Seligman let just anybody enter the contest."

Sizing up their competition, they strolled over to Hector, whose loose-leaf notebook was buzzing annoyingly.

"What is it?" Toni asked Hector.

"It's a privacy alarm," Hector explained proudly. "Anytime anybody closes my binder, a buzzer goes off."

"Hector." Toni laughed, closing and then opening Hector's loose-leaf. "That doesn't make sense."

"Why?" Hector asked, losing his smile.

"It should buzz when somebody tries to open it," Toni explained, "before somebody gets a chance to see what you've written."

"Oh," Hector said, looking concerned. "You're right."

"Listen," Toni said, putting the pillow gently down on Hector's seat. She ran her finger across some wires, tracing them from the binder cover to the buzzer. She glanced up at Maxine, then back to Hector.

"Look," she said, pointing to the connections between the alarm and the binder. "If you move this here"—she disconnected the wire on the cover—"and put this here"—she opened the binder and pointed to its rings—"you can get it to buzz when you open it."

Hector took the wires from Toni and considered her idea. "And then it would buzz when you opened it?" he asked.

"I think so," Toni guessed.

"Thanks!" Hector said. "I'm going to do that!"

Toni smiled contentedly and picked up the pillow. Maxine grabbed Toni's arm and pulled her aside.

"What are you doing?" Maxine asked angrily. "He's our competition!"

"You think some book that buzzes is going to beat us out? What competition?" Toni asked. She shook her head. "Maxine, we did it! We invented something that keeps away bad dreams. I can't wait to bring the award home to my grandmother. It's going to change everything."

"But the class votes on a winner," Maxine pointed out. "And nobody in the class likes us."

"Victor likes us," Toni joked.

"And who's going to listen to Victor?" Maxine asked.

"Hey, don't make fun of Victor. I've been talking to him. He doesn't have any friends. He lives in this burnt-out building on Woodhaven Boulevard, and I think he's waiting for some sort of invasion or something. And I think we're the only two people who were ever nice to him. He let me tutor him. He even tried one of your invention ideas. He entered the contest too."

"What?" Maxine was amazed. "What idea?"

"Something about chalk, chalk that sparkles or something."

"I can't believe it!" Maxine said.

"C'mon." Toni patted Maxine's back. "Nobody can compete against us. Look!" She pointed to Debbie.

Debbie was showing some girls her stick-on, peel-off lipstick. It looked as if she had applied different lipstick colors to pieces of Scotch tape, which she then stuck to her lips.

"Well, that's going to save a lot of lives," Toni said sarcastically.

"Oh, yeah?" Debbie snapped. "And what did you invent?"

"This." Toni beamed, holding up the pillow.

"That looks brilliant." Debbie smirked. "Nobody's ever invented a pillow before."

"It keeps away bad dreams," Maxine explained.

"Oh, yeah?" Debbie snickered. "The only thing that would keep away my bad dreams is having her"— Debbie pointed to Toni—"fall into a sewer."

"And see your family!" Toni snapped back. She picked up the pillow to hit Debbie over the head.

Maxine grabbed Toni's arms and dragged her away. "C'mon, calm down. That's our invention! Let's go set it up."

Mr. Seligman walked from team to team, examining each project. Maxine watched him smile and laugh as he leaned over Elisa's desk and read, or tried to read, something she had written. Maxine watched Shawnna take the paper from Mr. Seligman's hand and place it over a small bulb they had set up on the desk. The bulb was attached to a dry cell. Elisa pointed excitedly to the paper. Mr. Seligman drew back his head and opened his eyes dramatically. He applauded.

"You know, Maxine," Toni said quietly, smoothing out the pillow. "My mom is never coming back."

It sounded so strange, so bland, as if Toni were telling her some boring fact, something she was tired of worrying about. Not knowing what to say, Maxine looked up to watch Mr. Seligman examine Hector's loose-leaf binder alarm. He shook Hector's hand, then walked up to the chalkboard. On a long chart was a list of everybody's names and inventions. Next to each invention was a small box for the number of votes that entry received.

"I think it's time," Mr. Seligman said, "for each contestant to come up to the front and explain their invention."

"Toni," Maxine whispered, "your grandma's going to be really proud. She is. You give our presentation."

Shawnna and Elisa went first. Over Maxine's hissing, they received a round of polite applause. Hector went second. He was followed by Erik, then Debbie, then Victor, who went to the board and wrote in chalk,

A TANK IS AN ALL-PURPOSE VEHICLE.

When the class became as quiet as the chalk on the board, Victor turned to the class and apologized.

"It was supposed to sparkle," he said, staring at the ground.

Toni applauded enthusiastically.

Reading from the list on the board, Mr. Seligman called out, "The Pillow."

Toni took a deep breath and walked to the front of the room. After smiling nervously at Maxine, she began. "We invented our pillow," she said in a clear, proud voice, "to solve a problem. What could we create to prevent bad dreams?"

She explained how her grandmother had a hard time sleeping when the apartment was quiet. She told the class about Wat's problems at the doctor's and during nap time. She told them how she ran out into the street, wearing her pajamas, to call Maxine with her idea, and how Maxine put the pillow together in the middle of the night. She detailed how the pillow solved their problem.

When Toni finished, Maxine waited for the applause. After a moment of silence, Mr. Seligman cleared his throat and said, "All right, why don't we vote?"

Toni snuck back to her seat. Her face was red.

"What went wrong?" she whispered to Maxine.

"I don't know." Maxine shrugged.

One by one, the kids in the class voted. Maxine looked up at the board. Something strange was happening. As Mr. Seligman went around the room, quite a few of the kids voted for Shawnna and Elisa's invisible ink. But quite a few voted for "the Pillow" as well. It was hard to read Mr. Seligman's dashes. It was a two-person race. Maxine glanced over at Toni, who was also keeping a tally on a piece of paper.

Maxine asked, "Who's winning?"

"I can't believe it," Toni said.

Mr. Seligman called on Maxine.

"I vote for our pillow," she said proudly.

Then he called on Hector.

"I vote for the pillow," Hector declared.

Then Mr. Seligman called on Elisa.

"I vote for our ink." She giggled.

"We're down by one," Toni whispered to Maxine. "And there are two kids left."

Then Mr. Seligman called on Victor.

At first Victor didn't hear Mr. Seligman. He was fidgeting with his chalk, rubbing it against a piece of slate.

"Victor?" Mr. Seligman called.

Victor struck the chalk angrily at the slate.

"Victor? Who are you going to vote for?" Mr. Seligman asked.

Again Victor snapped the chalk against the slate.

"Victor?"

And then Victor blew up.

Everything became quiet. A terrible sulfur smell filled the room. Her eyes stinging, Maxine saw Victor enveloped in a cloud of shifting gray smoke. Suddenly she felt a frighteningly empty feeling inside.

"Victor!" Mr. Seligman shouted. "Are you all right?" Mr. Seligman waved his hands in front of him, as if he were trying to open a hole in the smoke. "Are you hurt?"

"Wow," Victor said, clearly delighted. "Wow."

The room filled with a sour, burnt smell.

"What happened?" Mr. Seligman asked.

"Wow, it worked," Victor said, examining the backs and fronts of his charcoal-coated hands. "It worked."

"It was supposed to sparkle," Maxine said, burying her face in her arms.

"Victor . . ." Mr. Seligman stammered, taking a few cautious steps forward. "Are you all right?"

"Yeah," Victor said, still grinning, his eyes wide open. "I vote for the pillow."

"Victor, what . . ." Mr. Seligman asked, "what happened?"

"What just happened," Toni said, grabbing Maxine's arm and pinching it, "is we won. I'm the last vote. I'm the only vote left. I vote for us. I vote for us. We won!" She jumped up out of her seat and shouted, "I vote for us! I vote for us!"

Slowly, the smoke began to clear.

# ☆ 18 ☆

# Murmurs

*October 25*

Her hands were filled with valves and ventricles, an artery, and a vena cava. Though she had taken them apart, Maxine had no idea how to put them back together. It was making her nervous. The pieces in her hand no longer resembled a heart.

"So, Maxine," Dr. Stone asked, "did you enter the Inventions of Children Contest?"

Maxine gently set the plastic parts of the model heart on a table and looked up at Dr. Stone, who was leaning over her brother, rubbing a gel on Wat's belly and chest. The gel would help the sound waves travel better to and from Wat's heart.

Maxine glanced over at her parents. They were standing a few feet back, talking softly to each other. Her father winked at Maxine and gave her a smile. They didn't seem concerned with the exam. Her parents looked like they were waiting in line at a bakery.

"So did you enter?" Dr. Stone repeated.

"Yes," Maxine said.

Dr. Stone pushed his thick glasses up on his nose. Holding his sticky hands in the air, he rubbed his thick beard on his shoulder.

"Good!" Dr. Stone exclaimed. "What was your invention?"

"That's it," Maxine said, pointing to the pillow on the swivel chair by the door. "But some kid in Jackson Heights invented a light bulb that uses radio waves instead of electricity. He won the district."

"Too bad," Dr. Stone said, glancing over at the pillow. "When I came across the application for the contest—my son got it from his school up in the Bronx—you were the first person I thought of."

"The application?" Maxine asked.

"Yes, for the Inventions of Children Contest," Dr. Stone said, gesturing to his nurse to start up the machine.

"You sent it?"

"I immediately thought of you, my favorite almost-inventor." Dr. Stone smiled. He began to fasten the tiny patches to Wat's chest that would hold the cables from the echocardiograph. "I always think of you when I think of inventions or any of this technological stuff." He waved his hand, showing off the machine.

So it was Dr. Stone, all along. That's why Phil had never written back to her. He had never written to her in the first place. What a fool she had been! Phil had never known she existed! Oh, she was so embarrassed! All those stupid letters!

"So what's so special about the pillow?" Dr. Stone asked.

"It keeps away bad dreams," Wat said, picking up his head. "And it smells nice. And it's got voices."

"It works?" Dr. Stone asked, sounding intrigued. "It's not an almost-works?"

"Yes," Wat said. "I used it at nap time so I wouldn't get arrested."

"It works," their father said proudly. "And it is a wonderful advance in . . . sleep technology. The best thing since counting sheep." He laughed.

"It keeps away bad dreams," Wat added.

"We thought, Dr. Stone," their mother said, "that perhaps Wat could rest his head on it while you examined him. Do you think that would be all right?"

"It doesn't blow up," Wat reassured everyone. "Her chalk blew up. It was supposed to sparkle, but it blew up."

"Well, let's see," Dr. Stone said, turning to the nurse. "What do you think, Dell?"

Dell, Dr. Stone's new nurse, was a small woman with a broad smile who had promised Wat she would tell him the story of the flying bears right after the exam. "You just think about what a flying bear could do," she had suggested to him. "Just think, while you're lying there, while we're doing this exam. Maybe you could help me with the story."

"I could think of a lot of things flying bears can do," Wat had told her.

"I think the pillow is an excellent idea," Dell said. "Perhaps if it works, we could borrow it for a few of our other child patients?" she asked Maxine.

"Sure! My friend Toni helped me invent it," Maxine said. "It . . . it was really her idea."

Dell picked up the pillow and pressed her nose against it. "It smells lovely," she told Maxine.

"It's from the stuff my mother sticks in Maxine's underwear drawer," Wat explained.

Maxine's mother laughed. So did her father.

"Well, let's give it a try," Dr. Stone said, and gently lifting Wat's head, slid the pillow beneath him.

Dell turned out the lights. Dr. Stone turned on the monitor of the echocardiograph.

Maxine prayed, "Please be a beautiful heart. Please be a beautiful heart."

And Wat lay quietly, as if he were fast asleep.

# ☆ **19** ☆

# A Guest Appearance

## *October 26*

Toni was late, but Maxine was not going to go to school without her. She pushed aside her bowl of cereal and removed her inventor's notebook and pencil from her book bag. It was a long walk for Toni. Maxine didn't mind waiting.

"Why are you staring into the refrigerator?" her mother asked her father. "It's not a major motion picture."

"What happened to the chicken that was in here?" Mr. Candle asked, searching the bottom shelf. "I wanted to have a piece for lunch."

"Ma," Maxine asked again, though she had heard the answer before, "it was just that Wat moved around too much during the first echocardiogram?"

"Yes," her mother said, pouring herself a cup of tea.

"All that time you said you weren't worrying, you were worrying?" Maxine asked.

Her mother shrugged. "Yes and no," she said. "We were *concerned*."

"We weren't worried," her father interrupted.

"You and Dad thought Wat was going to need an operation?"

"Well, it was a possibility," her mother said, leaning against the counter and sipping her tea. "When Wat moved around so much that time you weren't there, it made the echocardiogram difficult to read. The hole in his heart looked like it might have grown."

"And when Wat used my pillow," Maxine added eagerly, "the echocardiogram was better?"

"Yes," her mother said, pouring Wat's cereal. "It got Wat to lie still. It made the pictures much clearer. The hole hadn't grown. Dr. Stone said that nothing had changed in Wat's heart. The tiny hole is still just a tiny hole."

"He won't need an operation?" Maxine asked again. She needed to hear that answer over and over.

"No, he won't," her mother said.

Wat walked into the room. He sat down behind his bowl of cereal and his glass of juice with the Crazy Straw.

"Maxine," her mother said, walking over and putting her arms around her. "You are an inventor." She kissed the top of Maxine's head.

"Tell her what Dr. Stone said," Mr. Candle urged, still staring into the refrigerator.

"I told you," her mother reminded Maxine. "Dr. Stone wants to borrow your pillow to try it out with some other children. And I also told you that Dell wanted to buy it for herself." She laughed.

"Now what happened to the chicken that was in here?" Maxine's father asked, sounding more frustrated. He removed a can of soda and placed it on the floor next to a small collection of containers of food. "I just cooked that chicken yesterday."

"I brought it in for show-and-tell," Wat said, then took a sip from his Crazy Straw.

"A roasted chicken?" their father asked in disbelief. "You took a roasted chicken in for show-and-tell?"

Wat shrugged. "Yup."

Maxine laughed. Wat was going to be her brother forever. They were never going to give him back. She had invented something. She had invented something that would keep him with her. Feeling giddy, she watched the juice whirl and loop through Wat's straw into his mouth. She laughed again. She wished she had invented the Crazy Straw.

"An entire roasted chicken?" their mother asked, pouring herself another cup of tea. "Wat, you took an entire roasted chicken into school for show-and-tell?"

Wat nodded.

"How did you bring it to school?" their father asked.

"In my backpack," Wat said.

Their father brought a glass of milk and a bagel with him to the table. "What did Mrs. Finch say," their father asked Wat, "when you took a whole roasted chicken out of your backpack for show-and-tell?"

"She said I could go first."

"What did you do with it for show-and-tell?" their mother asked.

"I showed it," Wat said.

The phone rang. Their father stood up.

"I thought you were studying families," their mother asked, emptying the dregs of her cup into the sink. "How come you brought in a chicken?"

"Now we're studying animal families," Wat explained.

"Hello?" their father said into the phone. "Yes"—he looked at Maxine—"yes, she is."

Her mother turned to the phone. "Who is it?" she asked.

"Just a second," Mr. Candle said into the phone. Something had caught his eye. Something in the backyard. He covered the mouthpiece. "Maxine," her father said, peering out of the kitchen into their backyard, "I thought Wat was your paparazzo. Who did you get to take his place?"

Maxine didn't understand. She stared at Wat, then looked where her father was pointing. She didn't see anyone.

"I didn't see any camera, but I just saw some kid stick her head up right outside the window."

Maxine stood.

"I think I saw something red," her mother commented. "With glasses."

"Just a minute," her father said into the phone. "I'll have an answer for you in just a minute."

He walked to the back of the kitchen and opened the door.

"I was knocking on the front door, but nobody answered," Toni apologized, standing tall in a new red dress. "So I came around the back."

"Come in," Mr. Candle said.

"Hiya, Maxine, I'm sorry I'm late," she said, taking a step into the kitchen. "But ... but my grandmother ..." She smiled delightedly. "My grandmother overslept."

"She slept?" Maxine asked.

"She *over*slept," Toni corrected her.

"But I had the pillow," Maxine reminded her.

"But she had our certificate that said we won. She had it framed. She put it up above her bed."

"Come in, Toni," Maxine's mother said, pulling out a chair from the table. "You can join us for breakfast. Maybe Maxine's father could butter you a bagel. Would you like some juice?"

"No, thanks." Toni grinned. "My grandmother made me waffles." She walked over to the table and sat in Maxine's seat. "With syrup," she confided in Maxine. "And butter."

"I think I have another idea for an invention," Maxine said, turning the page of her notebook.

"Er ... Maxine"—her father covered the mouthpiece—"it's Phil Donahue's secretary. I think she wants to speak to you. Something about being a member of their studio audience. She's got two tickets."